乔伊斯作品中的
凯尔特歌谣

冯建明 等◎编译

The Celtic Songs and
Lyrics in Joyce's Works

上海三联书店

［编译著作说明页］

英汉双语编译著作《乔伊斯作品中的凯尔特歌谣》为教育部社会科学基金课题"2017 年度国别与区域研究中心（备案）：爱尔兰研究中心"（GQ17257）阶段性成果、上海对外经贸大学 2020 年"内涵建设-学位点建设-国际学术会议"最终成果、国际商务外语学院 2020 年度内涵建设计划任务最终成果。

本书主要由冯建明教授编纂、翻译、校对。

参加本书部分内容编纂、翻译、校对的成员：
刘翼桐、许荷影、秦宏、韩冰、张亚蕊

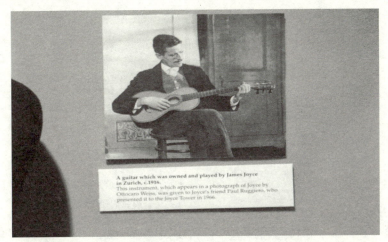

A guitar which was owned and played by James Joyce in Zurich, c.1916.
This instrument, which appears in a photograph of Joyce by Ottocaro Weiss, was given to Joyce's friend Paul Ruggiero, who presented it to the Joyce Tower in 1966.

曾被詹姆斯·乔伊斯拥有且约于 1916 年弹奏于苏黎世的一把吉他。

该照由奥托卡罗·韦斯拍摄。乔伊斯友人保罗·鲁吉罗曾得到该照片中的乐器,他在 1966 年把它赠给乔伊斯塔。

（上图由冯建明教授在 2014 年摄于乔伊斯塔内）

（2014 年,冯建明教授参观《尤利西斯》乔伊斯塔）

披睡衣的努沃莱塔

Nuvoletta in Her Light Dress

little cloud — Nuvoletta in her light dress
(Song Lyrics in Finnegans Wake)
nightdress — Nuvoletta in her light dress, by James Joyce
16 summers — spunn of sisteen shimmers,
was looking down on them,
bannisters — leaning over the bannistars
and list'ning all she childishly could.

...

She was alone.
cloud/lovely — All her nubied companions
were asleeping with the squir'ls.

...

She tried all the winsome wonsome ways
her four winds had taught her.
hazy, star — She tossed all her sfumastelliacinous hair
princess of Brittany — like la princesse de la Petite Bretagne
dainty — and she rounded her mignons arms
Mrs Patrick Campbell — like Missis Cornwallis-West
and she smiled over herself
like the image of the pose queen of the
Isolde of Ireland — of the daughter of the Emperour of Irelande
Tristan, sad, sadder — and she sighed after herself as were she born
demure young lady — to bride with Tristis Tristior ristissimus.
But, sweet madonnine, she might fair as well
have carried her daisy's worth to Florida.

...
Oh, how it was duusk. From Vallee Maraia to Grasyaplaina,
sleep — dormimust echo! Ah dew! Ah dew!
It was so duusk that the tears of night began to fall, ...
first by ones and twos, then by threes and fours,
at last by fives and sixes of sevens,
for the tired ones were weckning by the rain
as we weep now with them. O! O! Par la pluie!

Then Nuvoletta reflected for the last time
in her little long life myriadminded
and she made up all her myriads of drifting minds in one.
engagements — She cancelled all her engauzements.
bannisters — She climbed over the bannistars;
rain cloud — she gave a childy cloudy cry: Nuée! Nuée!
nightdress — A light dress fluttered.
She was gone.

披睡衣的努沃莱塔,

悠然自在十大夏,
曾俯视栏杆,
斜倚扶手,
相脱稚气,听万籁。

她曾形单影只。
她可爱的伙伴们
都正与那群松鼠同眠。

她曾试者用四风所授的
各种花式的绰约风姿
她像布列塔尼公主那样
甩了甩蓬松秀发,
如顽特里兄·坎沃尔·夫人一般
环抱娇美的双臂
她嫣然一笑,
模样妁妁,
爱尔兰的那位公主。
她焕然叹息,百结愁肠,
仿佛生当作特里斯坦新娘。
然而丽,婷婷,美丽的淑女含
心足活过此去佛罗里达。

噢,天色多以暗淡,山驿拉利谷到格拉西平达。
宏梦中的回声!啊,雨含!啊,雨含!
天色如此暗淡,夜雨始落,
先是初次,继而渐渐每次三四满,
最终每次五六七消,
由于那些疲倦者被炊少的湿,
此间我们正与其同哀。噢!哐!啦!随雨声少湿星!
然后,努沃莱塔在她智的人生阶段中
最后一次思索
她把她那漂浮的万千思绪聚成一体。
她取消所有约会。
她翻越越栏杆;
她如孩子般,发出啊妹期的儿减:雨含!雨云!
睡衣飘飘动。
她不见了。

目 录

编译者序

　　若谈论爱尔兰文化,必须参考爱尔兰文学。爱尔兰文学蕴含了爱尔兰文化。能完美表达爱尔兰文化的作家很多,而詹姆斯·乔伊斯(James Joyce,1882—1941)就是最典型的爱尔兰作家之一。故此,基于乔伊斯研究,上海对外经贸大学爱尔兰研究中心策划了如下作品的翻译和编译工作:

　　其一,译著系列之《斯蒂芬英雄:〈艺术家年轻时的写照〉初稿的一部分》(*Stephen Hero*:*Part of the first draft of A Portrait of the Artist as a Young Man*,1944)。《斯蒂芬英雄:〈艺术家年轻时的写照〉初稿的一部分》于2019年在上海三联书店出版。该书是欧洲文学巨匠詹姆斯·乔伊斯名著《艺术家年轻时的写照》(*A Portrait of the Artist as a Young Man*,1916,或译作《青年艺术家的画像》)第一版手稿的部分内容。《斯蒂芬英雄:〈艺术家年轻时的写照〉初稿的一部分》含十二个章节,是乔伊斯的自传性作品,以斯蒂芬·迪达勒斯的早期成长经历为主线,表现了具有主人公的诗人气质,刻画了他从孩提时期到成年阶段的身心成长过程,并涉及斯蒂芬的家人、朋友、男性和女性、都柏林生活和天主教艺术等,在叙述手法上,比最终出版的《艺术家年轻时的写照》更加生动、具体和详尽,尤其对研究乔伊斯和《艺术家年轻时的写照》具有重要学术价值。

　　文学是人性重塑的心灵史,它不会游离于文化话语体系之外。乔伊斯生活与创作的时代正是爱尔兰社会发生重大变革的时期,其作品《艺术家年轻时的写照》显示出了更多现代主义意味,它将意识流与现实主义的叙事手法糅合在一起,对文学发展带来了重要的影响。相信,《斯蒂芬英雄:〈艺术家年轻时的写照〉初稿的一部分》的翻译会进一步加深我国学界对《艺术家年轻时的写照》的研究。

　　其二,译著系列之《看守我兄长的人:詹姆斯·乔伊斯的早期生活》(*My Brother's Keeper*:*James Joyce's Early Years*,1958)。乔伊斯的作品充满了爱尔兰性或爱尔兰岛屿特质，对了解、欣赏、研究凯尔特文化积淀极为重要。要研究詹姆斯·乔伊斯，就需多了解该作家的生平。目前，《看守我兄长的人：詹姆斯·乔伊斯的早期生活》尚未有该书的汉语译文。相信，该书汉语译著的出版具有现实意义：将推动我国的乔伊斯研究，有益于我国爱尔兰研究，更加速国内高校的爱尔兰文学的教学。

《看守我兄长的人：詹姆斯·乔伊斯的早年生活》由詹姆斯·乔伊斯的胞弟斯坦尼斯劳斯·乔伊斯撰写，回忆了与其兄长共同度过的早年生活，是难得的传记性，对爱尔兰代表性小说家詹姆斯·乔伊斯弥足珍贵。该书由三位作家的成果组成：T.S.艾略特的"序言"、理查德·艾尔曼所写"介绍"和"注释"以及斯坦尼斯劳斯·乔伊斯所写的回忆录。该书由理查德·艾尔曼编辑。该回忆录分为"故土"、"萌芽"、"初春"、"成熟"和"初放"五部分。该书破解乔伊斯笔下人物原型之谜，揭示其故事情节的起源，探索了乔伊斯的原始材料被加工的程度和方法，把读者的兴趣延伸到乔伊斯的家庭、朋友、他在都柏林生活的每个细节和都柏林的地貌——这个承载着他孩童时期、青少年时期和青年时期的都柏林，帮助读者把握乔伊斯性格与其小说的联系，为研究爱尔兰作家提供一个独特视角。

其三，译著系列之《〈为芬尼根守灵〉析解》(*A Skeleton Key to Finnegans Wake*, 1947)。在乔伊斯的诸多作品中，《为芬尼根守灵》(*Finnegans Wake*, 1939)极其重要，被许多重要的评论家视为后现代主义的开山之作，它有助于研究西方现代主义，更是讨论后现代主义的珍贵资料。《为芬尼根守灵》十分重要，在诸多乔伊斯研究者眼中，它是乔伊斯的压轴之作；同时，它也被许多评论家视为后现代主义的范例，是研究西方后现代主义必不可少的佳作。

《〈为芬尼根守灵〉析解》是由约瑟夫·坎贝尔和亨利·莫顿·罗宾逊合作的经典力作，旨在揭开内容丰富性、寓意深刻，难以被暗示的《为芬尼根守灵》(或译作《芬尼根的守灵夜》)的神秘面纱。《〈为芬尼根守灵〉析解》的突出特点在于：简单扼要，显示最重要的主题，忠实于原作情节，其目的不是为了阐释哪一段或者哪个意象群，而是讲述该小说最基本的叙事内容。《为芬尼根守灵》现世后，坎贝尔和罗宾逊挖掘了暗藏于该小说的纲要，整理出关于该小说的众多评论，捋出《为芬尼根守灵》骨架结构的线索，将西欧文学巨子詹姆斯·乔伊斯梦幻般的复杂而惊奇的叙事展现出来，成为《为芬尼根守灵》及其重要的指南性著作。

其四，译著系列之《〈为芬尼根守灵〉普查：人物及其角色索引》(*A Census of Finnegans Wake：An Index of the Characters and Their Roles*，1956)。该书由艾德琳·格拉欣创作，分"前言"、"序言"、"概要"、"人物身份"、"勘误表"和"普查"六部分；其中，"前言"出自理查德·埃尔曼之手。此书是一部调查之作，向读者提供了破解西方现代主义和后现代主义大师詹姆斯·乔伊斯"天书"的才思，它又堪称《为芬尼根守灵》(或译作《芬尼根的守灵夜》)不可或缺的指南，列出该小说的几乎所有人物，涉及众多人名和多数人名标识的不同变形。《〈为芬尼根守灵〉普查：人物及其角色索引》并非只为《为芬尼根守灵》的专业研究者而备，它更为入门级读者提供参考。艾德琳·格拉欣以奇妙的撰写手法，化解了乔伊斯所创大量而迷人的难题，让读者备受启发而随她迎难而上，以便与大家分享《为芬尼根守灵》的无穷魅力。

《为芬尼根守灵》由 4 部分组成，目前，仅有该书第一部分的汉语译文，尚未出现全本汉语译文。《〈为芬尼根守灵〉析解》和《〈为芬尼根守灵〉普查：人物及其角色索引》从不同角度，对《为芬尼根守灵》进行了阐释、说明、讲解，是翻译《为芬尼根守灵》必不可少的重要资料。目前，《〈为芬尼根守灵〉析解》和《〈为芬尼根守灵〉普查：人物及其角色索引》尚没有汉译本。但愿，我们对它们的翻译能为研究《为芬尼根守灵》提供便利。

其五，译著系列之《流亡者》(*Exiles*，1918)。《流亡者》为三幕剧，是爱尔兰作家詹姆斯·乔伊斯创作的惟一剧作。该剧发生在都柏林郊区的梅林和拉尼拉格。该剧主人公是爱尔兰作家理查德·罗恩，他曾自我流放到意大利，于 1912 年夏天，携带与其私奔十年的情人柏莎，返回都柏林，作短暂逗留，并在此期间，爱上音乐教师比阿特丽斯·贾斯蒂斯。同时，柏莎则有意于记者罗伯特·汉德。这四个中年人虽有情，却难以沟通，彼此不理解。故此，无论在爱尔兰，还是在海外，他们都不断流亡。该剧除了这四个主要人物，还包含三个次要角色：罗恩与柏莎的儿子阿奇、罗恩家的女仆布里吉德和一个卖鱼妇。作为乔伊斯的惟一剧本，它虽然涉及的人物不多，却清晰描写出流亡者之间的情感纠葛。乔伊斯运用角色转换等手法，表现了现代爱尔兰人的焦虑感和异化感，凸显了 20 世纪初期西方社会流亡者的孤独感。

其六，译著系列之编译作品《乔伊斯作品中的凯尔特歌谣》(*The Celtic Songs*

and Lyrics in Joyce's Works）。《乔伊斯作品中的凯尔特歌谣》是英汉双语对照的歌谣编译成果，由可谱曲的诗歌与被吟唱的民歌或民谣组成。诗歌是最古老的文学样式，源于民歌或民谣。基于此，《乔伊斯作品中的凯尔特歌谣》可作为析解乔伊斯作品的一条重要线索，蕴含着爱尔兰非物质文化遗产的基本要素，展现了西方现代主义思潮与凯尔特传统互动的文学魅力，有助于打开一扇可欣赏"绿宝石岛"地域风情的迷人之窗。本书主要包含三大部分：被引用于乔伊斯叙事著作的凯尔特歌谣选段；用于乔伊斯作品的凯尔特歌谣典故；由乔伊斯创作的具有凯尔特魅力、可融诗歌于民乐的、在广义上能被视作民歌或民谣的《室内乐》和《为芬尼根守灵》等中的歌词。在乔伊斯作品中，凯尔特歌谣构成了情节发展和人物塑造的重要部分，揭示了凯尔特族群的多种理念，体现了现代主义叙事技巧的特质，见证了乔伊斯在诗歌创作上的尝试与探索，展示了民歌或民谣的民族性、口头性、集体性、地域性等特色。

在上述作品翻译和编译过程中，上海对外经贸大学爱尔兰研究中心主任牵头，为翻译团队成员提供基本资料，制定翻译和编译程序，提出翻译和编译要求，组织团队成员分工协作，定期完成翻译和编译任务。在翻译实践中，每隔一段时间，翻译团队成员进行讨论，解决翻译难题；翻译之后，团队成员再采用自校和互校结合的办法。该书汉语译文出版前，本课题负责人进行全文校对、修改、重译，撰写前言、后记、附录，负责出版事宜，根据出版社要求，反复修改、校稿、重译等。

当今，翻译领域存在多种翻译原则。对于上海对外经贸大学爱尔兰研究中心翻译团队，"忠实"与"可读"是最核心的翻译原则。对于译作，"忠实"不可或缺。在这里，本"译者序"不再进一步讨论翻译的"忠实"，而是聚焦"可读"。乔伊斯作品晦涩难懂，常被冠以"天书"二字，令人望而却步。与乔伊斯研究相关的作品难免涉及晦涩文字。基于"忠实"的"可读"看似容易，却对于乔伊斯作品翻译、乔伊斯评论及与乔伊斯研究相关的资料构成了挑战。

当今世界，乔伊斯研究已取得巨大成就，它为本研究团队的翻译提供了便利条件。尽管如此，对于说不尽的乔伊斯，乔伊斯研究并没有终结，它仍处于探索阶段。因此，本研究团队的译文难免存在缺陷。何况，团队协作之优劣同存，其劣势在于：尽管有统一校稿环节，在遣词习惯方面，团队译作仍不像出自一人手笔。本研究团队主要由任课教师和在读研究生组成，大家牺牲业余时间，不惧艰辛,进行了专业探索和笔译实践。

　　翻译可以让人体验艺术创造的美感。艺术创造永无止境。译文也不存在定式,更不存在"绝对的终稿",不会没有不可改进的余地。本人在翻译实践中,深刻感受到:在不同研究阶段,对译文措辞的选择存在着巨大的判断差异。在相对晚期的译作中,本人一旦有机会,就对曾在其它译作中翻译过的语句、句子、段落、诗篇等进行重译。故此,在本人负责翻译的不同译作中,相同的的语句、句子、段落、诗篇等并非具有相同的译文;在一定程度上,在本人负责翻译的这些译作中,相对后期出版的译作是对前期译作中某些语句、句子、段落、诗篇等的修正。例如,在译著系列之《斯蒂芬英雄:〈艺术家年轻时的写照〉初稿的一部分》中,有下列译文①:

　　　　　　　　ᶜ伴随着震颤的闹铃,黎明苏醒了,
　　　　　　　　灰白、阴冷、空旷!
　　　　　　　　哦,抓住我白色的手臂,环绕的手臂!
　　　　　　　　浓密的秀发,请将我隐藏!

　　　　　　　　生活是一场梦,一场梦。时间在消逝
　　　　　　　　诗歌被述说
　　　　　　　　我们从光明和太阳的谎言中走出
　　　　　　　　去向阴冷死亡的荒地。ᶜ

　　在译著系列之编译作品《乔伊斯作品中的凯尔特歌谣》中,依据原文,上述诗句则被重译为:

　　　　　　　　⁽约⁾伴着阵阵颤抖的铃声,黎明醒来,
　　　　　　　　　　何等灰暗,何等阴冷,何等空旷!
　　　　　　　　哦,用白色的双臂、环抱着的双臂搂住我吧!

----

① 见冯建明等译的《斯蒂芬英雄:〈艺术家年轻时的写照〉初稿的一部分》(上海:三联书店,2019年)第28页。

也用浓发遮挡我吧!

人生是一场梦,一场梦。那一小时的宗教仪式结束了
　　一小段赞美诗也被朗诵
　　我们从圣灵亮光和日光假象中走出
　　迈向死者那清冷的荒原。(约)

再如,在译著系列之《看守我兄长的人:詹姆斯·乔伊斯的早期生活》中,有下列译文①:

我傻抱着一线希望
你莫关窗
听见我徘徊
来这儿在歌唱,我的小姐?

在译著系列之编译作品《乔伊斯作品中的凯尔特歌谣》中,依据原文,上述四行诗句也被重译:

我能傻傻地期望
你开着窗
听着我在这儿徘徊
和唱歌吗,我的心上人?

另外,在本翻译团队的译著系列中,人名和地名主要依据郭国荣主编的《世界人名翻译大辞典》(北京:中国对外翻译出版社,1993年)和周定国主编的《外国地名译名手册》(中型本,北京:商务印书馆,1993年)。但是,对于译著系列之《〈为芬尼根守灵〉析解》和译著系列之《〈为芬尼根守灵〉普查:人物及其角色索

---

① 见冯建明等译的《看守我兄长的人:詹姆斯·乔伊斯的早期生活》(上海:上海三联书店,2019年)第78页。

引》中人名和地名的译文,当我们团队的译文与书林出版社编辑建议的译文相左时,我们一律尊重书林出版社编辑的意见,而采用书林出版社建议的译文。下面,就以若干英文姓名的译法为例(对于译著系列之《〈为芬尼根守灵〉析解》和译著系列之《〈为芬尼根守灵〉普查:人物及其角色索引》,书林出版社采用繁体汉字):

英文姓名	原译稿版	出版社版	英文姓名	原译稿版	出版社版
Beatrice	比阿特麗斯	碧翠絲	Niger	尼日爾	尼日
Brigid	布里吉德	布麗姬	Blake	布萊克	布雷克
Osiris	俄塞里斯	歐西里斯	Tiberius	提貝里乌斯	提比略
Woden	奥丁	沃登	Oedipus	俄狄浦斯	伊底帕斯
Stephen	斯蒂芬	史蒂芬	Thomas	托马斯	汤玛斯
Jones	瓊斯	鍾斯	Grace	格雷丝	葛蕾
Dion	戴恩	迪恩	Garry	加里	盖瑞
Finn	芬恩	费恩	Cleopatra	克莱奥帕特拉	克丽奥佩特拉
Gutenberg	古登堡	谷腾堡	Livingstone	利文斯通	李文斯顿
Hilary	希拉里	希拉瑞	Isaac	伊萨克	艾塞克
Jason	賈森	杰森	Dean	迪安	迪恩
Patrick	帕特里克	派翠克	Kinglake	金莱克	金雷克
Raglan	拉格倫	拉葛蘭	Bishop	毕晓普	毕肖普
Berry	貝里	貝瑞	Tristan	特里斯特拉姆	崔斯坦
Veronica	韋羅妮卡	维若妮卡	Aphrodite	阿佛洛狄忒	阿芙萝黛蒂
Madge	瑪奇	玛姬	Mendelssohn	门德爾松	孟德尔颂
Oliver	奥利佛	奥立佛	Humphrey	汉弗莱	韩福瑞
Midas	彌达斯	米达斯	MacCulloch	麥卡洛克	麦克库洛克
Sandy	桑迪	郝思蒂	Christopher	克里斯托弗	克里斯多夫
Hosty	郝思蒂	珊蒂	Charlotte	夏洛特	夏綠蒂
Maud	莫德	茉德	Gregorius	格里戈里厄斯	格列哥里
Steel	斯蒂爾	史提爾	Gregorian	格雷戈里安	格列哥里
Berkeley	伯克利	伯克莱	Kippure	基皮尔山	基普尔山
Reilly	歐赖莉	歐赖利	Dionysus	狄俄尼索斯	戴奥尼索斯

但愿，本研究团队的系列翻译成果（含编译成果）有抛砖引玉之功用，为未来乔伊斯作品的翻译和研究提供参考。

欢迎大家批评指正。本团队学人愿不断修订、改进译作和编译之作，与大家共同进步。

是为系列译作（含编译成果）之"译者序"。

冯建明

上海对外经贸大学

教育部国别与区域研究中心爱尔兰研究中心

2020 年冬

乔伊斯作品中的凯尔特歌谣

《室内乐》（1907）

I

Strings in the earth and air
    Make music sweet;
Strings by the river where
    The willows meet.

There's music along the river
    For Love wanders there,
Pale flowers on his mantle,
    Dark leaves on his hair.

All softly playing,
    With head to the music bent,
And fingers straying
    Upon an instrument.

1

地面和空中的一根根琴弦
　　奏出悦耳的乐曲；
河旁的一根根琴弦
　　拨动着一条条柳枝。

乐曲在河畔飘扬
　　只因爱神在此游荡，
浅色花朵挂上他的斗篷，
　　深色叶子落于他的发上。

如此轻柔地演奏，
　　低头陶醉于乐曲，
几根手指跳动
　　在一件乐器上。

II

The twilight turns from amethyst
    To deep and deeper blue，
The lamp fills with a pale green glow
    The trees of the avenue.

The old piano plays an air，
    Sedate and slow and gay；
She bends upon the yellow keys，
    Her head inclines this way.

Shy thought and grave wide eyes and hands
    That wander as they list —
The twilight turns to darker blue
    With lights of amethyst.

2

黄昏由淡紫色变成
　　愈来愈暗的蓝光，
路灯泛着淡绿色的光笼罩在
　　林荫道的一棵棵树上。

古老钢琴演奏一曲，
　　宁静、缓慢、愉悦；
她身向黄色琴键弯曲，
　　头向这边倾斜。

羞怯之心、严肃大眼和双手
　　有节奏地漫游着——
黄昏变成更深的蓝光
　　染着一道道淡紫色的光芒。

III

At that hour when all things have repose，
    O lonely watcher of the skies，
    Do you hear the night wind and the sighs
Of harps playing unto Love to unclose
    The pale gates of sunrise?

When all things repose，do you alone
    Awake to hear the sweet harps play
    To Love before him on his way，
And the night wind answering in antiphon
    Till night is overgone?

Play on，invisible harps，unto Love，
    Whose way in heaven is aglow
    At that hour when soft lights come and go，
Soft sweet music in the air above
    And in the earth below.

3

在万物已眠之时，
　　哦，孤独地遥望天空之人，
　　你是否听到晚风和
给爱神弹奏的阵阵竖琴的悲鸣
　　来打开那一扇扇朝霞的鱼肚白大门？

在万物安眠时，你是否独自醒来
　　聆听一把把竖琴的美妙之音
　　在他的旅途上，为他前面的爱神弹奏，
晚风吹拂与琴声和应
　　直至夜晚消失？

一把把无形的竖琴为爱神弹奏，
　　天堂里谁的路被照亮
　　在柔和的一束束光来往之时，
轻柔悦耳的乐声飘于上面的天空
　　也飘于下面的大地。

IV

When the shy star goes forth in heaven
    All maidenly, disconsolate,
Hear you amid the drowsy even
    One who is singing by your gate.
His song is softer than the dew
    And he is come to visit you.

O bend no more in revery
    When he at eventide is calling.
Nor muse: Who may this singer be
    Whose song about my heart is falling?
Know you by this, the lover's chant,
    'Tis I that am your visitant.

4

天空中，当那颗羞答答的星星
　　像少女忧郁地前行之时，
你听，在令人困倦的暮色中
　　某人在你门边唱歌。
他的歌声柔过露水
　　他只为看望你而来。

哦，黄昏时，当他在呼唤
　　莫再垂首苦想。
毋需沉思：唱歌的人会是谁
　　谁的歌声突然出现，触动了我的心？
凭此歌声认出你，那是爱人歌，
　　我就是要见你的人。

V

Lean out of the window,
　　Goldenhair,
I hear you singing
　　A merry air.

My book was closed,
　　I read no more,
Watching the fire dance
　　On the floor.

I have left my book,
　　I have left my room,
For I heard you singing
　　Through the gloom.

Singing and singing
　　A merry air,
Lean out of the window,
　　Goldenhair.

5

探出窗，
　　金发女孩，
我听到你在哼
　　一曲欢快的小调。

我合上一本书，
　　不再读它，
望着着地面上
　　火苗在跳跃。

我已放下书本，
　　离开自己的房间，
因为我透过暮色
　　听见你正哼着歌。

哼着，哼着
　　一曲欢快的小调，
探出窗，
　　金发女孩。

VI

I would in that sweet bosom be
    （O sweet it is and fair it is!）
Where no rude wind might visit me.
    Because of sad austerities
I would in that sweet bosom be.

I would be ever in that heart
    （O soft I knock and soft entreat her!）
Where only peace might be my part.
    Austerities were all the sweeter
So I were ever in that heart.

6

我愿在那迷人的胸怀
　　（啊，多么迷人，多么温和！）
那里没有狂风能折磨我。
　　　由于悲苦生活
我愿在那迷人的胸怀。

我愿长住那心里
　　（啊，我轻轻地敲，温柔地恳求她！）
在那里，惟有安宁与我相关。
　　　生活即使再苦也变甜
那么我会长住那心里。

VII

My love is in a light attire
    Among the apple-trees，
Where the gay winds do most desire
    To run in companies.

There，where the gay winds stay to woo
    The young leaves as they pass，
My love goes slowly，bending to
    Her shadow on the grass；

And where the sky's a pale blue cup
    Over the laughing land，
My love goes lightly，holding up
    Her dress with dainty hand.

7

我的爱人身着轻薄盛装
　　在那片苹果林中，
在那里，一阵阵欢快的风儿渴望
　　结伴而奔。

在那里，一阵阵欢快的风儿逗留追求
　　飘过的嫩叶，
我的爱人缓步而去，弯下腰
　　她的身影映于那片草地；

在那里，天空是一只淡蓝色的杯子
　　笼罩着带笑意的大地，
我的爱人轻步而去，
　　芊芊玉手支撑着她的衣裙。

VIII

Who goes amid the green wood
    With springtide all adorning her?
Who goes amid the merry green wood
    To make it merrier?

Who passes in the sunlight
    By ways that know the light footfall?
Who passes in the sweet sunlight
    With mien so virginal?

The ways of all the woodland
    Gleam with a soft and golden fire —
For whom does all the sunny woodland
    Carry so brave attire?

O，it is for my true love
    The woods their rich apparel wear —
O，it is for my own true love，
    That is so young and fair.

8

是谁走在绿林中
　　尽可能让春天装扮她？
是谁走在欢快的绿林中
　　让树林更加欢快？

是谁在阳光下
　　从熟知的一条条带着轻柔足音的路上走过？
是谁走在在甜蜜的阳光下
　　带着纯真的风采？

整个树林里一条条的路
　　闪着柔和的金色火光——
那整片洒满阳光的林地究竟为谁
　　身着如此华丽的衣衫？

哦，为我的真爱
　　一棵棵树身披盛装——
哦，为我自己的真爱，
　　她如此年轻又美丽。

IX

Winds of May，that dance on the sea，
Dancing a ring-around in glee
From furrow to furrow，while overhead
The foam flies up to be garlanded，
In silvery arches spanning the air，
Saw you my true love anywhere?
    Welladay! Welladay!
    For the winds of May!
Love is unhappy when love is away!

9

一阵阵五月风,在海上起舞,
欢快地绕着圈吹动
自波谷至波谷,头顶上面
那层泡沫扬起,形成环状花饰,
架在空中一扇扇银色拱门里,
可曾看见我的真爱何在?
　　唉!唉!
　　为五月那一阵阵的风!
当爱人离开,爱情则令人悲伤!

X

Bright cap and streamers，
    He sings in the hollow：
      Come follow，come follow，
        All you that love.
Leave dreams to the dreamers
    That will not after，
    That song and laughter
      Do nothing move.

With ribbons streaming
    He sings the bolder；
    In troop at his shoulder
      The wild bees hum.
And the time of dreaming
    Dreams is[①] over —
    As lover to lover，
      Sweetheart，I come.

---

① 编译者注：原文即如此。

10

色泽鲜艳的帽子和一条条飘带，
　　他常在那个小山谷中唱歌：
　　　　来追随，来追随，
　　　　　　你所爱的人。
把一场场梦留给那些梦中人吧
　　那些梦中人不会追随，
　　　　那歌曲及笑声
　　　　　　都令其无动于衷。

一条条丝带在飘动
　　他更加自信地唱歌；
　　成群的野蜂嗡嗡地叫着
　　　　　列成一排，在他的肩旁。
那做梦期间
　　梦已觉——
　　面向情侣，作为情侣，
　　　　亲爱的，我来了。

XI

Bid adieu, adieu, adieu,
    Bid adieu to girlish days,
Happy Love is come to woo
    Thee and woo thy girlish ways —
The zone that doth become thee fair,
The snood upon thy yellow hair.

When thou hast heard his name upon
    The bugles of the cherubim
Begin thou softly to unzone
    Thy girlish bosom unto him
And softly to undo the snood
That is the sign of maidenhood.

11

别了,别了,别了,

    向少女时代道别,

快乐的爱神就到了

    向你求爱,也追求你那少女时期的丰姿——

那条腰带让你变得漂亮,

那条发带则缠在你黄色发上。

当你在小天使那阵阵号声中

    听见他的名字

你开始轻柔地向他

    张开你那少女胸怀

轻轻解下那条发带

那是处女的标记。

XII[①]

What counsel has the hooded moon
　　Put in thy heart, my shyly sweet，
Of Love in ancient plenilune，
　　Glory and stars beneath his feet —
A sage that is but kith and kin
With the comedian Capuchin?

Believe me rather that am wise
　　In disregard of the divine，
A glory kindles in those eyes
　　Trembles to starlight. Mine，O Mine!
No more be tears in moon or mist
For thee，sweet sentimentalist.

① 此诗也见斯坦尼斯劳斯·乔伊斯所著《看守我兄长的人：詹姆斯·乔伊斯的早期生活》(My Brother's Keeper：James Joyce's Early Years，New York：The Viking Press，1958)第 151 页。此诗译文参见、引用冯建明等译的《斯蒂芬英雄：〈艺术家年轻时的写照〉初稿的一部分》(上海：三联书店,2019 年)第 138 页。

12

被笼罩的月亮把什么忠告

　　寄于你心，我羞涩的宝贝，

自古老盈月中的爱神，

　　他的双脚下是荣耀与群星——

一位圣贤也是亲朋

头戴有趣的连帽斗篷？

不如信我，我明察善断

　　无视牧师，

那些眼中闪着荣光

　　冲着星光颤动。我的宝贝，哦，我的宝贝！

在月下或薄雾里不再

为你流泪，多愁善感的宝贝。

XIII

Go seek her out all courteously,
    And say I come,
Wind of spices whose song is ever
    Epithalamium.
O, hurry over the dark lands
    And run upon the sea
For seas and lands shall not divide us
    My love and me.

Now, wind, of your good courtesy
    I pray you go,
And come into her little garden
    And sing at her window;
Singing: The bridal wind is blowing
    For Love is at his noon;
And soon will your true love be with you,
    Soon, O soon.

13

去,恭敬地把她请出来,
　　就说我来啦,
香风在唱
　　祝婚歌。
哦,快快走过那一片片黑土地
　　也在海面上疾驰
海域及陆地都不能把我们分离
　　我和我的爱人。

此刻,风啊,蒙你允许
　　我恳求你去,
进入她的小花园
　　在她窗旁唱歌;
唱着:新婚的风儿在吹动
　　爱神正值盛年;
不久,你的真爱会到你这来,
　　不久,哦,不久。

XIV

My dove, my beautiful one,
    Arise, arise!
    The night-dew lies
Upon my lips and eyes.

The odorous winds are weaving
    A music of sighs:
    Arise, arise,
My dove, my beautiful one!

I wait by the cedar tree,
    My sister, my love,
    White breast of the dove,
My breast shall be your bed.

The pale dew lies
    Like a veil on my head.
    My fair one, my fair dove,
Arise, arise!

14

我的鸽子啊，我的丽人，
　　起来吧，起来吧！
　　夜露洒在
我双唇及两眼上。

阵阵香风正在编织
　　一支充满叹息的乐曲：
　　起来吧，起来吧，
我的鸽子啊，我的丽人！

在雪松旁，我等着，
　　我妹妹，我爱人，
　　那只鸽子的白胸脯，
我的胸膛将是你的床。

白色露珠
　　像一层面纱罩在我头上。
　　我的美人啊，我美丽的鸽子啊，
起来吧，起来吧！

XV

From dewy dreams, my soul, arise,
 From love's deep slumber and from death,
For lo! the trees are full of sighs
 Whose leaves the morn admonisheth.

Eastward the gradual dawn prevails
 Where softly-burning fires appear,
Making to tremble all those veils
 Of grey and golden gossamer.

While sweetly, gently, secretly,
 The flowery bells of morn are stirred
And the wise choirs of faery
 Begin (innumerous!) to be heard.

15

从一场场短如朝露的梦中,我的灵魂,起来吧,
　　从爱的沉睡中,也从死亡状态中,
看啊! 树丛充满着叹息声
　　早晨的树叶在提醒。

黎明向东渐显
　　那儿的天空露出一簇微燃火苗,
使得一层层灰色和金色
　　的轻薄丝织面纱都在颤动。

芬芳地,轻柔地,悄悄地,
　　早晨,一座座饰以花卉图形的钟被摇动
诸多聪明小仙子的合唱团
　　开始(无数遍地!)唱歌。

XVI

O cool is the valley now
    And there, love, will we go
For many a choir is singing now
    Where Love did sometime go.
And hear you not the thrushes calling,
    Calling us away?
O cool and pleasant is the valley
    And there, love, will we stay.

16

哦,此刻那道溪谷好凉爽
　　亲爱的,我们去那儿吧
因为好多唱诗班正在歌唱
　　爱神也曾去过那儿。
难道你没听到那群画眉正啼鸣,
　　在呼唤我们动身?
哦,那道溪谷凉爽而怡人
　　亲爱的,我们在那儿驻足吧。

XVII

Because your voice was at my side
    I gave him pain，
Because within my hand I held
    Your hand again.

There is no word nor any sign
    Can make amend —
He is a stranger to me now
    Who was my friend.

17

因你的声音曾在我身旁回响
　　我让他受过痛伤，
因我曾把你的手
　　又一次握于我手掌。

无言也无兆
　　可补偿——
他曾是我友，
　　如今是路人。

XVIII

O sweetheart, hear you
    Your lover's tale;
A man shall have sorrow
    When friends him fail.

For he shall know then
    Friends be untrue
And a little ashes
    Their words come to.

But one unto him
    Will softly move
And softly woo him
    In ways of love.

His hand is under
    Her smooth round breast;
So he who has sorrow
    Shall have rest.

18

哦，亲爱的，你听听
　　你恋人的故事；
人会有忧伤
　　在他遭受群朋背弃时。

因为他届时就会意识到
　　诸友的不忠
他们的话化作
　　一小片灰烬。

但有一位向他
　　悄悄走近
并温柔地追求他
　　以爱的诸多方式。

他的手位于
　　她光滑而圆润的胸下；
他满怀忧伤
　　需要得到休养。

XIX

Be not sad because all men
    Prefer a lying clamour before you：
Sweetheart，be at peace again —
    Can they dishonour you?

They are sadder than all tears；
    Their lives ascend as a continual sigh.
Proudly answer to their tears：
    As they deny，deny.

19

莫因人人
　　爱对你撒谎喧闹而悲伤：
亲爱的，再冷静一下——
　　他们能令你蒙羞吗？

比起所有痛哭流涕的人，他们更加悲伤；
　　他们的生活化作了一声长叹。
骄傲地回应他们的泪水：
　　尽管他们不承认，不承认。

XX

In the dark pine-wood
  I would we lay,
In deep cool shadow
  At noon of day.

How sweet to lie there,
  Sweet to kiss,
Where the great pine-forest
  Enaisled is!

Thy kiss descending
  Sweeter were
With a soft tumult
  Of thy hair.

O, unto the pine-wood
  At noon of day
Come with me now,
  Sweet love, away.

20

在那幽暗的松林中
　　我愿我们躺下，
在成排而凉爽的树荫里
　　于正午时分。

躺在那儿多美妙，
　　亲吻多甜蜜，
在壮观的松林里
　　有狭长通道！

你那俯首之吻
　　会更甜蜜
伴着你那一缕披散
　　的柔发。

哦，朝着那松林
　　于正午时分
此刻就跟我来，
　　亲爱的人儿，走。

XXI

He who hath glory lost, nor hath
 Found any soul to fellow his,
Among his foes in scorn and wrath
 Holding to ancient nobleness,
That high unconsortable one —
His love is his companion.

21

他已丧失荣誉，仍未发现
　　　有人追随他，
满怀蔑视与愤怒，他身处敌群
　　　却坚守着古老贵族的尊严，
那高挑而落寞之人——
是他的爱人，也是他的伴侣。

XXII

Of that so sweet imprisonment
　　My soul, dearest, is fain —
Soft arms that woo me to relent
　　And woo me to detain.
Ah, could they ever hold me there
Gladly were I a prisoner!

Dearest, through interwoven arms
　　By love made tremulous,
That night allures me where alarms
　　Nowise may trouble us;
But sleep to dreamier sleep be wed
Where soul with soul lies prisoned.

22

对于那如此惬意的禁锢

　　我的内心，最亲爱的，欣然接受——

温柔的双臂使我不再拒绝

　　使我留下。

啊，愿它们能把我长留在那儿

我希望做一名爱的囚徒！

最亲爱的，凭借一条条交织的手臂

　　因爱而导致战栗，

夜色吸引我，那儿的阵阵闹铃声

　　丝毫不能干扰我们；

然而睡眠时间与美妙睡眠相伴

在那儿，心灵禁锢着心灵。

XXIII

This heart that flutters near my heart
    My hope and all my riches is,
Unhappy when we draw apart
    And happy between kiss and kiss:
My hope and all my riches — yes! —
And all my happiness.

For there, as in some mossy nest
    The wrens will divers treasures keep,
I laid those treasures I possessed
    Ere that mine eyes had learned to weep.
Shall we not be as wise as they
Though love live but a day?

在我心旁跳动的这颗心
　　就是我的希望和所有财富，
我们离别时会忧伤
　　一吻再吻时则感到愉悦：
我的希望和所有财富——是的！——
还有我的所有幸福。

在那儿，如同在某个布满苔藓的巢穴
　　那群鹪鹩会存放潜鸟的珍宝，
我存放我拥有的那些珍宝
　　在我双目学会哀悼之前。
难道我们不会与它们同样聪明
虽然爱情仅存一天？

XXIV

Silently she's combing,
    Combing her long hair
Silently and graciously,
    With many a pretty air.

The sun is in the willow leaves
    And on the dappled grass,
And still she's combing her long hair
    Before the looking-glass.

I pray you, cease to comb out,
    Comb out your long hair,
For I have heard of witchery
    Under a pretty air,

That makes as one thing to the lover
    Staying and going hence,
All fair, with many a pretty air
    And many a negligence.

24

她正安静地梳妆，
　　梳着她的长发
安静而优雅，
　　带着多种可爱神态。

阳光照进那层层的柳叶
　　也照在那片有斑影的草地，
而她依旧在镜前
　　梳着长发。

我恳求你，停下梳理，
　　梳理你那长发，
因为我听说过魔法
　　在可爱的神态下，

会使因此而
　　留下和离开的恋人，
都一样，带着多种可爱神态
　　和各式漫不经心。

XXV

Lightly come or lightly go:
    Though thy heart presage thee woe,
Vales and many a wasted sun,
    Oread let thy laughter run,
Till the irreverent mountain air
Ripple all thy flying hair.

Lightly, lightly — ever so:
    Clouds that wrap the vales below
At the hour of evenstar
    Lowliest attendants are;
Love and laughter song-confessed
When the heart is heaviest.

25

轻轻而来或轻轻而去：
　　虽然你的心可预感你会悲哀，
山岳女神让你的笑声穿过，
　　一道道山谷和未被利用的阳光，
直到那无礼的山风
吹皱你那满头飘发。

轻轻地，轻轻地——总是如此：
　　在暮星照耀之时
朵朵白云笼罩下面的一道道山谷
　　是最卑贱的仆从；
当心情最沉重时，
以歌示爱与笑。

XXVI

Thou leanest to the shell of night，
    Dear lady，a divining ear.
In that soft choiring of delight
    What sound hath made thy heart to fear?
Seemed it of rivers rushing forth
From the grey deserts of the north?

That mood of thine，O timorous，
    Is his，if thou but scan it well，
Who a mad tale bequeaths to us
    At ghosting hour conjurable —
And all for some strange name he read
In Purchas or in Holinshed.

26

你向那夜之壳，
　　亲爱的女士，侧着一只探听的耳朵。
在那轻柔而令人愉快的合唱中
　　什么音乐令你敬畏？
好似一条条河流向前奔淌
源于北方那一片片的灰色沙漠？

你那心情，唔，羞羞答答的，
　　与他的一样，只要你细思量，
他在施魔法那段时间
　　给我们留下一则令人痴迷的传说——
而都因他在珀切斯或霍林希德的文中
读到某一怪名。

XXVII

Though I thy Mithridates were，
    Framed to defy the poison-dart，
Yet must thou fold me unaware
    To know the rapture of thy heart，
And I but render and confess
The malice of thy tenderness.

For elegant and antique phrase，
    Dearest，my lips wax all too wise；
Nor have I known a love whose praise
    Our piping poets solemnize，
Neither a love where may not be
Ever so little falsity.

27

即使我是你的万能解药，
　　制出以对抗那毒镖，
但你必须拥抱我
　　勿使我察觉你那内心狂喜，
而我仅回报和承认
你那温柔恶行。

若要说优雅而古老的字眼，
　　最亲爱的，我的双唇变得不善言辞；
我尚不知有一种爱
　　被我们那群诗人庄严高歌，
也不懂有一种爱
竟被掺入那么多虚情。

XXVIII

Gentle lady, do not sing
    Sad songs about the end of love;
Lay aside sadness and sing
    How love that passes is enough.

Sing about the long deep sleep
    Of lovers that are dead, and how
In the grave all love shall sleep:
    Love is aweary now.

28

温柔的女士，莫唱
　　一首首爱意之终的悲歌；
搁置忧伤，歌唱
　　爱意逝去方式则足矣。

歌唱已故恋人们
　　那长久的沉睡
爱意如何在墓中尽将归寂：
　　此刻爱神已倦。

XXIX

Dear heart, why will you use me so?
    Dear eyes that gently me upbraid,
Still are you beautiful — but O,
    How is your beauty raimented!

Through the clear mirror of your eyes,
    Through the soft sigh of kiss to kiss,
Desolate winds assail with cries
    The shadowy garden where love is.

And soon shall love dissolved be
    When over us the wild winds blow —
But you, dear love, too dear to me,
    Alas! why will you use me so?

29

亲爱的，你为何这般待我？
    温柔嗔怪我的迷人双眸，
你美丽依旧——但，哦，
    你的美丽竟妆扮如此！

透过你那清澈如镜的双眸，
    穿过一吻再吻之间的轻叹，
阵阵凄风呼啸而袭
    多荫的花园是爱情处所。

爱情很快会消散
    当阵阵狂风从我们身旁吹过——
而你，亲爱的，我的挚爱，
    唉！你为何这般待我？

XXX

Love came to us in time gone by
 When one at twilight shyly played
And one in fear was standing nigh —
 For Love at first is all afraid.

We were grave lovers. Love is past
 That had his sweet hours many a one；
Welcome to us now at the last
 The ways that we shall go upon.

30

爱情于昔日来过我们身旁
　　当时，一人在暮色中腼腆地玩耍
还有一人在不远处提心吊胆地站着——
　　因为爱情起初让人十分害怕。

我们曾是严肃的情侣。爱情已逝
　　许多人有过甜蜜时光；
最终，欢迎立刻来到我们身旁
　　我们将继续前行。

XXXI

O, it was out by Donnycarney
　　When the bat flew from tree to tree
My love and I did walk together;
　　And sweet were the words she said to me.

Along with us the summer wind
　　Went murmuring — O, happily! —
But softer than the breath of summer
　　Was the kiss she gave to me.

31

噢,那是在东尼演艺团外
　　蝙蝠在一棵棵树间飞舞
我和我爱人一起散步;
　　她对我讲着甜蜜话语。

夏风与我们相伴
　　一路喃喃细语——啊,多么快乐!——
但比那夏季微风更柔和的
　　是她那曾给我的一吻。

XXXII

Rain has fallen all the day.
    O come among the laden trees：
The leaves lie thick upon the way
    Of memories.

Staying a little by the way
    Of memories shall we depart.
Come，my beloved，where I may
    Speak to your heart.

32

雨已洒落一整天。
哦，来此载满果实的树丛中：
那充满回忆的路
被覆盖上一层层树叶。

通过系列回忆而停留
片刻，我们将会离开。
来吧，我的心上人，我可在此
与此话衷肠。

XXXIII

Now, O now, in this brown land
    Where Love did so sweet music make
We two shall wander, hand in hand,
    Forbearing for old friendship' sake,
Nor grieve because our love was gay
Which now is ended in this way.

A rogue in red and yellow dress
    Is knocking, knocking at the tree;
And all around our loneliness
    The wind is whistling merrily.
The leaves — they do not sigh at all
When the year takes them in the fall.

Now, O now, we hear no more
    The vilanelle and roundelay!
Yet will we kiss, sweetheart, before
    We take sad leave at close of day.
Grieve not, sweetheart, for anything —
The year, the year is gathering.

33

此刻，啊此刻，在这片褐色土地上
　　爱神演奏过那么甜美的音乐
我俩将手挽着手漫步，
　　出于昔日友情而克制，
不会因我们的爱情曾充满欢乐
如今以此方式告终而悲。

一个身着红黄衣服的无赖
　　正敲击，敲击着那棵树；
在我们孤独的四周
　　那风在欢快地呼啸。
当一年时光在秋季带走叶片时
那一片片叶子——它们并未悲鸣。

此刻，啊此刻，我们再也听不见
　　维拉内拉曲和回旋曲！
亲爱的，我们在黄昏伤别前
　　仍会亲吻。
亲爱的，莫为任何事情悲伤——
时光飞逝，年复一年。

XXXIV

Sleep now, O sleep now,
    O you unquiet heart!
A voice crying "Sleep now"
    Is heard in my heart.

The voice of the winter
    Is heard at the door.
O sleep, for the winter
    Is crying "Sleep no more."

My kiss will give peace now
    And quiet to your heart —
Sleep on in peace now,
O you unquiet heart!

34

马上睡吧,喂,马上睡吧,
　　喂,你那不安宁的心!
一种"马上睡吧"的呼喊声
　　在我心中回荡。

冬之声
　　在门旁回荡。
喂,睡吧,因为冬季
　　在呼喊"莫再睡了"。

此刻,我的一吻准会给
　　你的内心以平和与安宁——
此刻,继续安宁地睡吧,
喂,你那不安宁的心!

XXXV

All day I hear the noise of waters
　　　Making moan,
Sad as the sea-bird is, when going
　　　Forth alone,
He hears the winds cry to the waters'
　　　Monotone.

The grey winds, the cold winds are blowing
　　　Where I go.
I hear the noise of many waters
　　　Far below.
All day, all night, I hear them flowing
　　　To and fro.

35

我整日听到海水
　　发出悲叹，
悲伤得犹如那海鸟
　　孤独前行之时，
他听到一阵阵风伴着那
　　单调的海浪声而哭泣。

一阵阵阴风、一阵阵寒风正吹向
　　我所到之处。
我听到下方远处
　　重重海浪的喧闹。
我整日、整夜听到它们
　　往复涌流。

XXXVI

I hear an army charging upon the land,
    And the thunder of horses plunging, foam about their knees:
Arrogant, in black armour, behind them stand,
    Disdaining the reins, with fluttering whips, the charioteers.

They cry unto the night their battle-name:
    I moan in sleep when I hear afar their whirling laughter.
They cleave the gloom of dreams, a blinding flame,
    Clanging, clanging upon the heart as upon an anvil.

They come shaking in triumph their long, green hair:
    They come out of the sea and run shouting by the shore.
My heart, have you no wisdom thus to despair?
    My love, my love, my love, why have you left me alone?

36

我听到一队人马在此地冲锋，
　　群马入水，如雷轰鸣，水花溅膝：
御车夫们骄傲自大，身着黑甲，立于马后，
　　蔑视缰绳，挥动皮鞭。

他们对着夜空呼喊战斗口号：
　　我在梦中呻吟，这时，远远听到他们那一连串的笑声。
他们像一道炫目的火焰，劈开诸梦的幽暗，
　　叮叮当当，叮叮当当，像敲击一个铁砧那样，打在人心上。

他们得意洋洋，颤动着绿色长发而来：
　　他们从海上来，在岸边连跑带吼。
我的心上人，难道你会因无才而绝望？
　　我的爱人，我的爱人，我的爱人，你为什么丢下我不管？

《都柏林人》(1914)中的歌谣

The Song of Fionnuala[①]

Silent, oh Moyle, be the roar of thy water,
Break not, ye breezes, your chain of repose,
While, murmuring mournfully, Lir's lonely daughter
Tells to the night-star her tale of woes.
When shall the swan, her death-note singing,
Sleep, with wings in darkness furl'd?
When will heav'n, its sweet bell ringing,
Call my spirit from this stormy world?

Sadly, oh Moyle, to thy winter-wave weeping,
Fate bids me languish long ages away;
Yet still in her darkness doth Erin lie sleeping,
Still doth the pure light its dawning delay.
When will that day-star, mildly springing,
Warm our isle with peace and love?
When will heav'n, its sweet bell ringing,
Call my spirit to the fields above?

---

① 作为典故,此歌谣出现于《都柏林人》之《两个浪子》,其作者为托马斯·莫尔(Thomas Moore,
1779—1852)。

菲奥诺拉之歌

哦,莫伊尔,让你那咆哮的波涛沉寂吧,
那一阵阵微风折不断你的憩息锁链,
李尔那孤独的女儿在忧伤地低语
向夜之星倾诉她的悲惨故事。
啼啭死亡音符的天鹅,何时才会阖起双翅,
在黑暗中入睡?
天堂悦耳的钟声何时敲响,
把我的灵魂从这个风暴世界召回?

哦,莫伊尔,命运使我长期丧失活力,
令我面朝你那冬季的浪涛而伤心地哭泣;
而艾琳仍躺在黑暗中睡眠,
纯洁之光依然延迟来临。
启明星何时会冉冉升起,
用和平与关爱温暖我们的小岛?
天堂悦耳的钟声何时敲响,
把我的灵魂召至岸上的田野?

The Gipsy Girl's Dream①

I dreamt that I dwelt in marble halls，
With vassals and serfs at my side，
And of all who assembled within those walls，
That I was the hope and the pride.

I had riches too great to count，could boast
Of a high ancestral name；
But I also dreamt，which pleased me most，
That you lov'd me still the same ...

That you lov'd me，you lov'd me still the same，
That you lov'd me，you lov'd me still the same.

I dreamt that suitors sought my hand；
That knights upon bended knee，
And with vows no maiden heart could withstand，
They pledg'd their faith to me；

And I dreamt that one of that noble host
Came forth my hand to claim.
But I also dreamt，which charmed me most，
That you lov'd me still the same ...

That you lov'd me，you lov'd me still the same，
That you lov'd me，you lov'd me still the same.

---

① 作为典故，此歌谣出现于《都柏林人》之《泥土》，其作者为艾尔弗雷德・邦恩（Alfred Bunn，
1796—1860）。

吉普赛女孩的梦

我曾梦见自己住在大理石府邸，
有多位家臣和农奴相伴左右，
对于那些聚在围墙内的人们，
我是他们的希望和骄傲。

我曾拥有数不清的财富，可炫耀
一个显赫家世；
而我也梦到你曾依然爱我，
这最令我愉悦⋯⋯

你爱过我，你曾依然爱我，
你爱过我，你曾依然爱我。

我曾梦见求婚者们想牵我的手；
还有一个个骑士单腿屈膝，
立下多项令任何少女无法拒绝的誓约，
他们承诺对我忠贞不渝；

我还梦到其中一位高贵的求婚者
前来要牵我的手。
而我也梦到你曾依然爱我，
这最令我着迷⋯⋯

你爱过我，你曾依然爱我，
你爱过我，你曾依然爱我。

I'll sing thee songs of Araby^①

I'll sing thee songs of Araby
And tales of fair Cashmere,
Wild tales to cheat thee of a sigh
Or charm thee to a tear.
And dreams of delight shall on thee break
And rainbow visions rise,
And all my soul shall strive to wake
Sweet wonder in thine eyes ...
And all my soul shall strive to wake
Sweet wonder in thine eyes.

Through those twin lakes where wonder wakes
My raptured song shall sink
And, as the diver dives for pearls,
Bring tears, bright tears, to their brink.
And dreams of delight shall on thee break
And rainbow visions rise,
And all my soul shall strive to wake
Sweet wonder in thine eyes ...
And all my soul shall strive to wake
Sweet wonder in thine eyes.

---

① 作为典故,此歌谣出现于《都柏林人》之《阿拉比》,其作者为威廉·戈尔曼·威尔斯(William Gorman Wills, 1828—1891)。

我要给你唱几首阿拉比之歌

我要给你唱几首阿拉比之歌
还有关于克什米尔集市的种种传说，
许多荒唐故事骗你发出一声叹息
抑或迷惑你淌出一滴泪。
你的一系列美梦将破灭
呈现出五彩缤纷的幻象，
我整个灵魂将努力唤醒
你双目中的美好奇迹……
我整个灵魂将努力唤醒
你双目中的美好奇迹。

穿过那唤醒奇迹的双子湖
我销魂的歌声将消失
恰似潜水员们寻觅一颗颗珍珠，
把一串串泪珠、一串串明亮的泪珠，带至双子湖岸。
你的一系列美梦将破灭
呈现出五彩缤纷的幻象，
我整个灵魂将努力唤醒
你双目中的美好奇迹……
我整个灵魂将努力唤醒
你双目中的美好奇迹。

Yes, Let Me Like a Soldier Fall[①]

Yes! Let me like a Soldier fall,
Upon some open plain,
This breast expanding for the ball
To blot out ev'ry stain.
Brave manly hearts confer my doom
That gentler ones may tell
Howe'er forgot, unknown my tomb,
    I like a Soldier fell.
Howe'er forgot, unknown my tomb,
I like a Soldier fell.
    I like a Soldier fell.

I only ask of that proud race,
Which ends its blaze in me,
To die the last, and not disgrace
Its ancient chivalry!
Tho' o'er my clay no banner wave,
Nor trumpet requiem swell,
Enough they murmur o'er my grave
    He like a Soldier fell.
Enough they murmur o'er my grave
    He like a Soldier fell.
    He like a Soldier fell.

---

① 作为典故,此歌谣出现于《都柏林人》之《死者》,其作者为爱德华·菲茨伯尔(Edward Fitzball,
1792—1873)。

对,让我像战士一样倒下

对！让我像战士一样倒下，

在某一开阔的平原上，

这个胸膛为子弹敞开

以便抹去每一处污点。

一颗颗勇敢而阳刚的心赋予我死亡的权力

较温和的人们也许会说

无论是否忘却,不知道我坟墓在何处,

　　　我像战士一样倒下。

无论是否忘却,不知道我坟墓在何处,

　　　我像战士一样倒下。

我像战士一样倒下。

我只渴求那令人自豪的民族精神,

在我身躯内彻底燃烧,

直到战死,也不辱没

那古老的骑士精神！

虽然我的躯体之上没有旗帜飘扬,

也没有安魂曲被小号奏响,

但已无憾,只要他们在我墓前低语

　　　他像战士一样倒下。

但已无憾,只要他们在我墓前低语

　　　他像战士一样倒下。

　　　他像战士一样倒下。

Killarney[①]

By Killarney's lakes and fells emerald isles and winding bays
mountain pass and woodland dells mem'ry ever fondly strays
bounteous nature loves all lands beauty wanders everywhere
footprint leaves on many strands but her home is surely there
angels fold their wings and rest in that Eden of the West
Beauty's home Killarney ever fair Killarney

Innis Fallen's ruined shrine may suggest a passing sigh
but man's faith can ne'er decline such God's wonders floating by
Castle Lough and Glena Bay Mountains Tore and eagle's nest
still a muckcross you must pray though the monks are now at rest
Angels wonder not that man there would fain prolong life's span
Beauty's home Killarney ever fair Killarney

Noplace else can charm the eye with such bright and varied tints
Ev'ry rock that you pass by verder 'boider or besprints
Virgin there the green grass grows，ev'ry morn springs natal day
bright hued berries daft the snows smiling winter's frown away
Angels often pausing there doubt if Eden were more fair
Beauty's home Killarney ever fair Killarney

---

① 作为典故，此歌谣出现于《都柏林人》之《艺术家年轻时的写照》，其作者为埃德蒙·福尔科纳
（Edmund Falconer, 1814—1879）。

基拉尼

在基拉尼的诸多湖泊、丘陵、翠绿小岛和蜿蜒海湾旁
在山口和林区中一道道小溪谷旁，回忆曾深情地游荡
慷慨的大自然热爱所有土地，美人则四处徘徊
脚印留在许多岸堤，但那里必定是她的家园
天使们收起双翅，在西方伊甸园休憩
美丽的家园基拉尼，永远美丽的基拉尼

伊尼斯福伦岛破败不堪的圣地可能暗示着一声轻叹
人类的信仰却从未婉拒神的一个又一个奇观飘过
城堡湖、格莱纳德湾特勒山脉、鹰巢
还有马克罗斯大教堂。即使修道士们现在正休息，你也须祈祷
天使们不诧异于那里的人会渴望延年益寿
美丽的家园基拉尼，永远美丽的基拉尼

别处无法以如此鲜艳而丰富的色彩吸引目光
你走过的每一块岩石都点缀或渲染
生长绿草的处女地，每天早晨都是春季新生之日
色彩鲜艳的浆果让积雪露出笑脸，使冬天舒展双眉
众天使常在那驻足，怀疑伊甸园是否更具魅力
美丽的家园基拉尼，永远美丽的基拉尼

Music there for echo dwells make each sound a harmony

Many voiced the chorus swells tillit faint in ecstacy

With the charmful tints below seems the Heaven above to vie

All rich colours that we know tinge the cloud wreaths in that sky

Wings of Angels so might shine glancing back soft light devine

Beauty's home Killarney ever fair Killarney

乔伊斯作品中的
凯 尔 特 歌 谣

那里的乐曲久久回荡,声声和谐
异口同声的合唱曲愈加响亮,直至令人喜极而晕
世间凭迷魅色彩引发高高在上的天堂争美
我们所知的斑斓色彩粉饰了云朵,为天空戴上花环
众天使那一对对如此有力的翅膀闪闪发亮,反射着柔和的圣光
美丽的家园基拉尼,永远美丽的基拉尼

Oh! Ye Dead①

Oh, ye Dead! Oh, ye Dead! whom we know by the light you give

From your cold gleaming eyes,

Tho' you move like men who live,

Why leave you thus your graves,

in far off seas and waves,

Where the worm and the seabird only know your bed.

To haunt this spot, where all

Those eyes that wept your fall,

And the hearts that wailed you like your own, lie dead!

It is true, It is true, We are shadows cold and wan;

And the fair, and the brave whom we loved on earth are gone,

But still thus ev'n in death,

So sweet the living breath

Of the fields and the flow'rs in our youth we wander'd o'er,

That ere, condemn'd, we go,

To freeze 'mid Hecla's snow,

We would taste it awhile, and think we live once more!

---

① 作为典故，此歌谣出现于《都柏林人》，其作者为托马斯·莫尔（Thomas Moore，1779—1852）。

哦！死者

哦，死者！哦，死者！我们了解你们，凭借你们所传递的眼神
通过你们那一双双冰冷闪光的眼睛，
尽管你们像活着的男人们那样移动，
你们为何要以此方式离开一座座坟墓，
到遥远的海洋和一片片波涛里，
在那些区域，蠕虫和海鸟知道你们的海底。
要常去此处，在此所有
那些眼睛曾为你们的阵亡而流泪，
像诸君之心那样哀悼诸君的一颗颗心纷纷丧失知觉！

的确如此，的确如此，我们是一个个冰冷而朦胧的影子；
我们在世上曾爱过的那些美人和勇士都去世了，
然而，即使我们死了，
我们年轻时曾漫步过的田野与朵朵花儿
仍会散发出芬芳的生命气息，
该死的，我们去世前，
去冰冷的赫克拉雪地，
我们愿感受积雪片刻，而想象自己多活一次！

The Lass That Loves a Sailor^①

The moon on the ocean was dimmed by a ripple

Affording a chequered delight;

The gay jolly tars passed a word for the tipple,

And the toast — for 'twas Saturday night:

Some sweetheart or wife he loved as his life

Each drank, and wished he could hail her:

But the standing toast that pleased the most

Was "The wind that blows,

The Ship that goes,

And the lass that loves a sailor!"

Some drank "The Queen," and some her brave ships,

And some "The Constitution";

Some "May our foes, and all such rips,

Yield to English resolution!"

That fate might bless some Poll or Bess,

And that they soon might hail her:

But the standing toast that pleased the most

Was "The wind that blows,

The Ship that goes,

And the lass that loves a sailor!"

Some drank "The Prince," and some "Our Land,"

This glorious land of freedom!

Some that our tars may never stand

---

① 作为典故，此歌谣出现于《都柏林人》，其作者为查尔斯·迪布丁（Charles Dibdin, 1745—
  1814）。

爱上一名水手的姑娘

海洋上空的月亮在一道波纹中略显暗淡
给人以一种无常乐趣；
那些寻欢作乐的水手曾给烈酒起了个绰号，
干杯——因为那是周末之夜：
他曾如命一般爱过的某位情人或妻子
每次饮酒，就想要他对其欢呼：
但常听到的最令人高兴的祝酒辞
是"那阵吹拂的风，
那条驶离的船，
还有那个爱上一名水手的姑娘！"

有些人为"女王"干杯，也有些人为她冒险乘帆，
还有些人维护"宪法"；
有些人高呼"愿我们的一个个仇敌和放荡之人，
屈从于英格兰人的决心！"
愿好运伴随某位波尔或贝丝，
而他们很快会向她致敬：
但常听到的最令人高兴的祝酒辞
是"那阵吹拂的风，
那条驶离的船，
还有那个爱上一名水手的姑娘！"

有些人为"王子"干杯，也有些人为"我们的国家，"
这个光荣的自由国度而战！
有些人可能让我们的水手们永不喜欢

For heroes brave to lead them!
That she who's in distress may find,
Such friends as ne'er will fail her.
But the standing toast that pleased the most
Was "The wind that blows,
The Ship that goes,
And the lass that loves a sailor!"

因为一位又一位英雄往往不顾危险而给他们带路！

危难中的她就会发现，

像这样的朋友永远不会舍弃她。

但常听到的最令人高兴的祝酒辞

是"那阵吹拂的风，

那条驶离的船，

还有那个爱上一名水手的姑娘！"

The Lass of Aughrim[①]

If you'll be the lass of Aughrim
As I am taking you mean to be
Tell me the first token
That passed between you and me.

REFRAIN
The rain falls on my yellow locks
And the dew it wets my skin;
My babe lies cold within my arms;
Lord Gregory let me in.

Oh Gregory, don't you remember
One night on the hill,
When we swapped rings off each other's hands,
Sorely against my will?
Mine was of the beaten gold
Yours was but black tin.

Oh if you be the lass of Aughrim,
As I suppose you not to be,
Come tell me the last token
Between you and me.

Oh Gregory don't you remember
One night on the hill,
When we swapped smocks off each other's backs,

---

① 作为典故,此诗出现于《都柏林人》,是一首爱尔兰民谣。

那个奥格里姆女孩

你若就是那个奥格里姆女孩
正如我想你会是她
对我说出吧
我和你之间传递的第一件信物。

副歌
雨水落在我那一绺绺黄发上
露水打湿了我的皮肤;
我的美人儿冷冰冰地躺在我怀中;
格雷戈里夫人,让我进去吧。

哦,格雷戈里,你难道不记得
在小山上的一个夜晚,
当时,我们交换了彼此手上的戒指,
这会极大地违背我的意愿?
我的是黄金的
你的只是黑锡的。

哦,你若是那个奥格里姆女孩
正如我估计你不会是她,
来吧,对我说出
我和你之间的最后信物。

哦,格雷戈里,你难道不记得
在小山上的一个夜晚,
当时,我们交换了彼此背上的罩衣,

Sorely against my will?
Mine was of the holland fine,
Yours was but Scotch cloth.

Oh if you be the lass of Aughrim,
As I suppose you not to be,
Come tell me the last token
Between you and me.

Oh Gregory, don't you remember,
In my father's hall.
When you had your will of me?
And that was the worst of all.

这会极大地违背我的意愿?
我的是优质荷兰亚麻布的,
你的只是苏格兰布料的。

哦,你若是那个奥格里姆女孩,
正如我估计你不会是她,
来吧,对我说出
我和你之间的最后信物。

哦,格雷戈里,你难道不记得,
在我父亲的会客厅里。
当时,关于我,你说出了自己的心愿?
结果,那是最糟糕的。

《艺术家年轻时的写照》(1916)中的歌谣

"从前,那可是一段美好时光,有一头牛沿着路走来了……"歌谣由约翰·斯坦尼斯劳斯·乔伊斯讲给幼年的詹姆斯·乔伊斯。詹姆斯·乔伊斯成人后,以该歌谣为其自传性小说的开头。1931 年 1 月 31 日,约翰·斯坦尼斯劳斯·乔伊斯在给詹姆斯·乔伊斯即将到来的生日贺信中提到:"我不知道,你是否还记得那段住在布赖顿广场的日子? 那时,你就是塔库娃娃,而我曾常将你带到那个广场,给你讲牛的故事。那头牛从山上下来,把小男孩带去。"以上引文出自 Morris Beja, ed. , *James Joyce*:*"Dubliners" and "A Portrait of the Artist as a Young Man"* (London:The MacMillan Press Ltd. , 1973),73.

在《艺术家年轻时的写照》①开篇,乔伊斯引语了这曲优美的凯尔特歌谣,并通过如下英语文字,使得凯尔特歌谣②与童真情趣联系起来:

Once upon a time and a very good time it was there was a moocow coming down along the road and this moocow that was coming down along the road met a nicens little boy named baby tuckoo. . . .

His father told him that story:his father looked at him through a glass:he had a hairy face.

He was baby tuckoo. The moocow came down the road where Betty Byrne lived:she sold lemon platt.

O,*the wild rose blossoms*

On the little green place.

He sang that song. That was his song.

O,*the green wothe botheth.*

When you wet the bed first it is warm then it gets cold. His mother put on the oilsheet. That had the queer smell.

His mother had a nicer smell than his father. She played on the piano the sailor's hornpipe for him to dance. He danced:

---

① James Joyce, *A Portrait of the Artist as a Young Man. The Portable James Joyce*. Ed. Harry Levin (New York:Penguin Books, 1976),245.

② 见本页斜体英文。

从前,那可是一段美好时光,有一头牛沿着路走来了,这头牛走着走着,遇到一个乖乖的小男孩,这个小男孩叫塔库娃娃……

　　他的父亲给他讲过那个故事;他的父亲透过一只单片眼镜瞅着他;他长着一个毛绒绒的脸。

　　他就是塔库娃娃。牛从贝蒂·伯恩家旁的路上走下来:她卖柠檬麻花糖。

　　哦,野玫瑰开放
　　在那一小片绿地上。

　　他唱那首歌。那首他的歌。

　　哦,那绿树下。

　　当你尿床了,先感到温,后觉着凉。他母亲铺上油布。油布有怪味。

　　他母亲身上的味比他父亲身上的味好闻。她弹钢琴,奏出水手角笛舞曲,为他跳舞伴奏。他跳着:

Tralala lala,
Tralala tralaladdy
Tralala lala,
Tralala lala.
...

绰啦啦　　啦啦

绰啦啦　　绰啦啦嘀

绰啦啦　　啦啦

绰啦啦　　啦啦①

……

---

① 该部分的译文和评论参见、引用冯建明：《乔伊斯长篇小说人物塑造》（北京：人民文学出版
　 社，2010 年）第 20 页。

Oft, in the Stilly Night (Scotch Air) [①]

Oft, in the stilly night,

Ere Slumber's chain has bound me,

Fond Memory brings the light

Of other days around me;

The smiles, the tears,

Of boyhood's years,

The words of love then spoken;

The eyes that shone,

Now dimm'd and gone,

The cheerful hearts now broken!

Thus, in the stilly night,

Ere Slumber's chain hath bound me,

Sad Memory brings the light

Of other days around me.

When I remember all

The friends, so link'd together,

I've seen around me fall

Like leaves in wintry weather;

I feel like one,

Who treads alone

Some banquet-hall deserted,

Whose lights are fled,

Whose garlands dead,

And all but he departed!

---

① 作为典故,此歌谣出现于《艺术家年轻时的写照》,其作者为托马斯·莫尔(Thomas Moore, 1779—1852)。

时常，在此寂静的夜晚(苏格兰小调)

时常，在此寂静的夜晚，
睡神的锁链捆住我之前，
美好回忆会带来
我那些往日时光；
少年时代的，
那一个个微笑、一串串眼泪
那时说出的爱的诺言；
目光曾闪闪发亮，
现在则黯淡而无光，
一种种愉快的心情现已破碎！
因而，在此寂静的夜晚，
睡神的锁链捆住我之前，
伤感回忆会带来
我那往日时光。

当我想起所有的
那些相处过的朋友，
我见过周围的人们去世
像冬天的一片片落叶；
我孤身只影，
孑然独行于
某个空荡荡的宴会大厅，
大厅的群灯已灭，
大厅的一堆花环枯萎，
而除他以外，众人皆离！

Thus, in the stilly night,
Ere Slumber's chain hath bound me,
Sad Memory brings the light
Of other days around me.

从而，在此寂静的夜晚，
睡神的锁链捆住我之前，
伤感回忆会带来
我那往日时光。

Brigid's Song①

Dingdong! The castle bell!

Farewell, my mother!

Bury me in the old churchyard

Beside my eldest brother.

My coffin shall be black,

Six angels at my back,

Two to sing and two to pray

And two to carry my soul away.

---

① 作为典故，此歌谣出现于《艺术家年轻时的写照》，其灵感源于一首诗，献给凯尔特女神布里吉德。

布里吉德之歌

叮当！那座城堡的钟声！
别了，我的母亲！
把我葬在那古老的教堂墓地吧
在我大哥身旁。
我的棺材要黑的，
六位天使雕像立于我身后，
两位唱歌，另两位祈祷
还有两位带走我的灵魂。

Sweet Rosie O'Grady[①]

Just down around the corner
of the street where I reside,
There lives the cutest little girl
that I have ever spied;
Her name is Rose O'Grady and,
I don't mind telling you,
That she's the sweetest little Rose
the garden ever grew.

    Sweet Rosie O'Grady,
    My dear little Rose,
    She's my steady lady,
    Most ev'ryone knows.
    And, when we are married,
    How happy we'll be;
    I love sweet Rosie O'Grady,
    And Rosie O'Grady loves me.

I never shall forget the day
she promised to be mine,
As we sat telling love tales
in the golden summer time.
'Twas on her finger that I placed
a small engagement ring,
While in the trees, the little birds

---

① 作为典故，此歌谣出现于《艺术家年轻时的写照》和《为芬尼根守灵》，其作者为莫德·纽金特
（Maude Nugent，1874—1958）。

可爱的罗茜·奥格雷迪

就在我居住的
街道拐角，
住着一位我所见过的
最可爱的小姑娘；
她名叫罗丝·奥格雷迪，
我不介意告诉你，
她是那座花园中曾长出的
最可爱的小玫瑰。

可爱的罗茜·奥格雷迪，
我亲爱的小罗丝，
几乎每人都知道，
她一直都是我的心上人。
而我们结婚后，
我们会多么幸福；
我爱可爱的罗茜·奥格雷迪，
罗茜·奥格雷迪也爱我。

我将永远忘不了那一天
她当时答应做我妻子，
在那美好的夏日时光
我们坐着讲述一个个爱情故事。
就在她的那根手指上，我戴上
一枚小小的订婚戒指，
与此同时，林中的一群小鸟

this song they seemed to sing!

Sweet Rosie O'Grady,

My dear little Rose,

She's my steady lady,

Most ev'ryone knows.

And when we are married,

How happy we'll be;

I love sweet Rosie O'Grady,

And Rosie O'Grady loves me.

乔 伊 斯 作 品 中 的
凯 尔 特 歌 谣

好像在唱这首歌！

可爱的罗茜·奥格雷迪，
我亲爱的小罗丝，
几乎每人都知道，
她一直都是我的心上人。
而我们结婚后，
我们会多么幸福；
我爱可爱的罗茜·奥格雷迪，
罗茜·奥格雷迪也爱我。

Oh Twine Me a Bower[①]

Oh twine me a bow'r all of woodbine and roses,

Far, far from the path of your commonplace joys;

Where the gem of contentment in silence reposes

Unsullied by tears and unshaken by noise.

Yes there would I dwell, in my own flow'ry cell

Nor the dream of ambition, of honour, or power,

Should tempt me to part from my own happy bower,

Should tempt me to part from my own happy bower.

True friendship should light up his torch at my dwelling

To cheer me when youth and its pleasures were past;

Without friends where on earth are the joys worth telling,

For friendship thro' years and thro' sorrows will last.

Yes there would I dwell, in my own flow'ry cell

Nor the dream of ambition of honour or power

Should tempt me to part from my own happy bower,

Should tempt me to part from my own happy bower.

---

① 作为典故，此歌谣出现于《艺术家年轻时的写照》，其作者为托马斯·克罗夫顿·克罗克
(Thomas Crofton Croker, 1798—1854)。

嘿，给我搭建一间农舍

嘿，给我搭建一间铺满忍冬和玫瑰的农舍，
远远地，远远地离开你们那平凡乐事之路；
在那里，憩息于寂静而令人满足的处所
不被一串串泪水而沾，不为喧嚣所撼。
一点不假，我愿住在那儿，就在我自己的花房
对抱负、荣誉和权力的渴望都不，
会诱使我离开我自己那快乐农舍，
会诱使我离开我自己那快乐农舍。

真正的友谊会在我的居所点亮他的火炬
当青春和其诸多乐趣逝去，给我慰藉；
没有众友，那一件件乐事究竟值得何处讲述，
因为经历多年和种种不幸的友谊将会持久。
一点不假，我愿住在那儿，就在我自己的花房
对抱负、荣誉和权力的渴望都不
会诱使我离开我自己那快乐农舍，
会诱使我离开我自己那快乐农舍。

The Groves of Blarney[①]

The Groves of Blarney they look so charming,
All by the murmuring of sweet silent streams,
Being banked with posies that spontaneous grow there,
Planted in order by the sweet Rockclose.
'Tis there's the daisy and sweet carnation,
The blooming pink, and the rose so fair;
The daffydowndilly, likewise the jilly-flowers
That scent the sweet fragrant air.
Oh! Oh! Och hone!

'Tis lady Jeffris that owns this station
Like Alexander or Queen Helen fair;
There's no commander through the nation,
For emulation can with her compare.
She has castles around her that no nine pounder
Should dare to plunder her place of strength;
But Oliver Cromwell he did her pummel,
And made a breach in her battlement.
Oh! Oh! Och hone!

'Tis there's the kitchen hangs many a flitch in,
With the maids a stitching upon the stair;
The bread and biskey, the beer and whiskey
Would make us frisky if we were there.
'Tis there you'd see Peg Murphy's daughter

---

① 作为典故,此歌谣出现于《艺术家年轻时的写照》和《为芬尼根守灵》,其作者为理查德·艾尔弗雷德·米利金(Richard Alfred Millikin, 1767—1815)。

| 乔伊斯作品中的
凯 尔 特 歌 谣

布拉尼的一片片小树林

布拉尼的一片片小树林显得很迷人，
都靠近发出潺潺水声的一条条纯净而安谧的小溪，
被堆堆自然生长在那儿的小花束点缀，
整齐地排列在不远处那可爱的岩石旁。
那里有雏菊，也有可爱的康乃馨，
有盛开的石竹，还有很美的玫瑰；
有水仙，也有百合，群芳
使空气中弥漫着芳香。
哦！哦！哎呀！

杰弗里斯女士坐拥有这片林地
像亚历山大，或如王后海伦那般漂亮；
遍及全国，没有任何指挥官，
可以与她相提并论。
她有多座城堡拱卫，应该没有重炮
敢被用于洗劫她的场所；
但奥利弗·克伦威尔却向她发起猛攻，
在她的城垛上开了一个缺口。
哦！哦！哎呀！

厨房中挂着好多腌熏猪肋条肉，
女仆们则在楼梯上缝衣；
我们若在那儿，看到面包加饼干，还有啤酒加威士忌
会使我们痛痛快快。
在那儿，你会见到佩格·墨菲女儿

A-washing pratees forenent the door
With Roger Cleary and Father Healy
All blood relations to Lord Donoughmore.
Oh! Oh! Och hone!

There's statues gracing this noble place in
Of heathen goddesses so fair:
Bold Neptune, Plutarch, and Nicodemus,
All standing naked in the open air.
So now to finish this brave narration
Which my poor geni could not entwine,
But were I Homer, or Nebuchadnezzar,
'Tis in every feature I would make it shine.
Oh! Oh! Och hone!

正在门前一边洗衣，一边与
罗杰·克利里和希利神父聊天
都与多诺莫尔勋爵有血缘关系。
哦！哦！哎呀！

有一些十分美丽的异教女神雕像
令此宏伟场所生辉：
轮廓清晰的海神、普卢塔尔克、尼科迪默斯，
都赤身裸体地露天而立。
现在，为了结束此篇需要勇气的叙述
我愚钝的天资无法赘述，
然而，我若是荷马或尼布甲尼撒，
我愿让此叙述中的每个特征都散发光芒。
哦！哦！哎呀！

Lily Dale[①]

As I hear the Mocking birds, I remember the words

When you said, that forever you'd love me

Now happiness is gone, memories linger on

From the chains of our love, I set you free

Sweet as the morning, smile like the sunshine

Ours was a love no words could tell

I love you, oh how I miss you

Won't you come back, Lily Dale?

Since we have said good bye, I'm so blue, I could cry

Happiness is a thing called the past

Days without you, make my nights, oh, so blue

And always in my heart, our love will last

Sweet as the morning, smile like the sunshine

Ours was a love no words could tell

I love you, oh how I miss you

Won't you come back, Lily Dale

Won't you come back, Lily Dale?

---

① 作为典故,此歌谣出现于《艺术家年轻时的写照》,其作者为亨利 S. 汤普森(Henry S. Thompson)。

莉莉·戴尔

我听到多只反舌鸟鸣啭时,回想起那些话
当时,你说会永远爱我
现在,幸福一去不复返,一串回忆滞留在
我们诸多爱的枷锁,我让你获得自由

惬意如晨,微笑似阳光
我们的爱无以言表
我爱你,哦,我多么想念你
莉莉·戴尔,你不回来吗?

自从我们道别后,我就很悲伤,我真想哭
幸福是昔日的事情
没有你的一天天,让我在一个个夜晚,哦,心情如此低落
一直以来,在我心中,我们的爱会持久不变

惬意如晨,微笑似阳光
我们的爱无以言表
我爱你,哦,我多么想念你
莉莉·戴尔,你不回来吗?
莉莉·戴尔,你不回来吗?

Suite of Stephen's Piano Improvisations[①]

The Agincourt Carol

Deo gratias Anglia redde pro victoria!

Owre Kynge went forth to Normandy

With grace and myght of chyvalry

Ther God for hym wrought mervelusly;

Wherefore Englonde may call and cry

CHORUS：

Deo gratias！

Deo gratias Anglia redde pro victoria！

He sette sege，forsothe to say，

To Harflu towne with ryal aray；

That toune he wan and made afray

That Fraunce shal rewe tyl domesday.

Chorus

Deo gratias！

Deo gratias Anglia redde pro victoria！

Then went hym forth，owre king comely，

In Agincourt feld he faught manly；

Throw grace of God most marvelsuly，

He had both feld and victory.

Chorus

Deo gratias！

Deo gratias Anglia redde pro victoria！

---

① 作为典故，此歌谣出现于《艺术家年轻时的写照》，其作者为拉尔夫·里奇(Ralph Richey)。

斯蒂芬的钢琴即兴演奏组曲

阿金库尔颂歌

感谢上帝,上帝将胜利赐予英格兰!
奥瑞·金吉去了诺曼底
带着优雅和高贵的气质
神之颂歌美妙无比;
为英格兰欢呼呐喊

副歌:
感谢上帝!
上帝将胜利赐予英格兰!
于是,他表示要围攻,
率领皇家军队,围攻哈弗勒尔镇;
在这里,他大获全胜,令敌人闻风丧胆
将统治法国直至地老天荒。

副歌
感谢上帝!
上帝将胜利赐予英格兰!
接着唱着赞美诗,哦,英俊的国王,
在阿金库尔战场上,他打起仗来刚劲有力;
绝妙地展示了上帝恩典,
他占领了阵地,并取得胜利。

副歌
感谢上帝!
上帝将胜利赐予英格兰!

Ther lordys, erles and barone
Were slayne and taken and that full soon,
Ans summe were broght into Lundone
With joye and blisse and gret renone.

Chorus
Deo gratias!
Deo gratias Anglia redde pro victoria!
Almighty God he keep owre kynge,
His peple, and alle his well-wyllynge,
And give them grace wythoute endyng;
Then may we call and savely syng:

Deo Gratias!
Deo Gratias Anglia Redde Pro Victoria!
Deo Gratias Anglia Redde Pro Victoria!

他们的那些勋爵、伯爵和男爵

很快被杀或被掳去，

而其中一些，连同成功、极乐和名誉

被带至伦敦。

副歌

感谢上帝！

上帝将胜利赐予英格兰！

万能上帝庇护吾王、

其民及其良愿，

施泽众生而永无止尽；

然，吾辈高呼而雅歌：

感谢上帝！

上帝将胜利赐予英格兰！

上帝将胜利赐予英格兰！

Greensleeves[①]

Alas，my love，you do me wrong,
To cast me off discourteously.
For I have loved you well and long,
Delighting in your company.

Chorus
Greensleeves was all my joy
Greensleeves was my delight，
Greensleeves was my heart of gold，
And who but my lady Greensleeves.

Your vows you've broken，like my heart，
Oh，why did you so enrapture me?
Now I remain in a world apart
But my heart remains in captivity.

Chorus
I have been ready at your hand，
To grant whatever you would crave，
I have both wagered life and land，
Your love and good-will for to have.

Chorus
If you intend thus to disdain，
It does the more enrapture me，
And even so，I still remain

---

① 作为典故,此诗出现于《艺术家年轻时的写照》和《斯蒂芬英雄》,是一首英国民谣。

绿袖女郎

哎，我的爱人，你委屈我了，
把我狠心抛弃。
我早已深爱你，
在你身旁，我心欢喜。

副歌
绿袖女郎是我欢乐的全部
绿袖女郎是我的欣喜，
绿袖女郎是我金子般的心，
我的绿袖女郎何人能及。

你打破了誓言，如同打碎我心，
哦，你为什么曾令我如此痴狂？
现在，我人虽仍在被分离的世界
我心却依然被囚。

副歌
我已准备在你左右，
准予你的一切恳求，
我已把生命和土地做赌注，
以便博得你的爱意和善意。

副歌
你若因此意欲鄙夷，
会令我愈加痴迷，
即便如此，我仍会做

A lover in captivity.

Chorus

My men were clothed all in green,

And they did ever wait on thee;

All this was gallant to be seen,

And yet thou wouldst not love me.

Chorus

Thou couldst desire no earthly thing,

but still thou hadst it readily.

Thy music still to play and sing;

And yet thou wouldst not love me.

Chorus

Well, I will pray to God on high,

that thou my constancy mayst see,

And that yet once before I die,

Thou wilt vouchsafe to love me.

Chorus

Ah, Greensleeves, now farewell, adieu,

To God I pray to prosper thee,

For I am still thy lover true,

Come once again and love me.

一名爱情俘虏。

副歌
我的男仆们都曾身着绿装，
他们的确曾等候你；
这一切都显示了骑士风度，
而你却对我不动情。

副歌
以前，你虽不会渴望尘世的一切，
却仍本可将其轻易拥有。
你那乐曲仍在弹唱，
而你却对我不动情。

副歌
好啦，我要祈求上天的神，
让你明白我始终如一，
并在我死前，仅仅一次，
你愿把爱惠赐予我。

副歌
啊，绿袖女郎，从现在起，别了，再会，
我祈求神赐福你，
因为我依然是你的真挚爱人，
归来吧，爱上我。

《尤利西斯》(1922)中的歌谣

Bronze by Gold Heard the Hoofirons, Steelyringing①

(Song Lyrics in *Ulysses by James Joyce*)

Bronze by gold heard the hoofirons, steelyringing.

Imperthnthn thnthnthn.

Chips, picking chips off rocky thumbnail, chips.

Horrid! And gold flushed more.

A husky fifenote blew.

Blew. Blue bloom is on the.

Gold pinnacled hair.

---

① 这些词语由乔伊斯创作，是《尤利西斯》第 11 章《赛壬》开篇中的文字，无标题，虽然相当于该
章提纲的部分内容，但具有自由诗的形式，且表达了诗歌意境，可作为现代主义形式的诗句。

一头褐发挨着一头金发听到蹄铁声，钢铁鏦鏦

（詹姆斯·乔伊斯小说《尤利西斯》中的诗句）

一头褐发挨着一头金发听到蹄铁声，钢铁鏦鏦。

粗粗粗、横横横。

一堆碎屑，从硬邦邦的拇指甲上扣下指甲屑，一堆碎屑。

真讨厌！金发的脸涨得更红。

一只横笛吹出嘶哑之声。

吹。一朵蓝花戴在。

高耸的金色发髻上。

Prrprr[①]

(Song Lyrics in *Ulysses by James Joyce*)

Prrprr.

Must be the bur.

Fff! Oo. Rrpr.

Nations of the earth.

No-one behind. She's passed.

Then and not till then.

Tram. Kran, kran, kran.

Good oppor. Coming.

Krandlkrankran.

I'm sure it's the burgund.

Yes. One, two.

Let my epitaph be.

Kraaaaaa.

Written. I have.

Pprrpffrrppffff.

Done. [②]

---

① 这些词语由乔伊斯创作,是《尤利西斯》第 11 章《赛壬》结尾中的文字,无标题,其原文的第四行至十四行为散文形式。这些词语表达了诗歌意境,可作为现代主义形式的诗句。

② 参见和引用冯建明:《乔伊斯长篇小说人物塑造》(北京:人民文学出版社,2010 年)第 123—124 页。

噗噗①

（詹姆斯·乔伊斯小说《尤利西斯》中的诗句）

噗噗。

一定是那杯勃艮第在捣蛋。

呼呼呼！噢噢。啰噗。

地上的万国。

背后没人。她过去了。

那时候才开始。

电车。喀隆，喀隆，喀隆。

恰好。来了。

喀隆咚喀隆咚喀隆。

我确定是那杯勃艮第在捣蛋。

嗯。一、二。

让人为我。

喀喇喇喇喇喇喇。

写碑文。我已说。

噗噗噗呼呼噗噗呼呼呼。

完。

---

① 该诗歌译文和注释引用冯建明：《乔伊斯长篇小说人物塑造》（北京：人民文学出版社，2010年）第126—127页。原文中，乔伊斯描写了布卢姆的意识流：

（1）他阅读着罗伯特·埃米特生命最后时刻的话："……地上的万国。那时候才开始，让人为我写碑文。我已说完。"作者特意用了斜体字描写了这部分。

（2）布卢姆想放屁原因："准是勃艮第……我肯定那杯勃艮第。嗯。"

（3）他还惦记着那个女士："背后没人。她过去了。"

（4）他对路过的电车的反应："恰好。来了。"

（5）他想着放屁的时机："一、二。"

这里的声音包含两种：

（1）布卢姆放的屁："噗噗……呼呼呼！噢噢。啰噗……噗噗噗呼呼噗噗呼呼呼。"

（2）行驶中的电车声："喀隆，喀隆，喀隆……喀隆咚喀隆咚喀隆……喀喇喇喇喇喇。"

Love's Old Sweet Song[①]

Once in the dear dead days beyond recall,
When on the world the mists began to fall,
Out of the dreams that rose in happy throng
Low to our hearts Love sang an old sweet song;
And in the dusk where fell the firelight gleam,
Softly it wove itself into our dream.

Just a song at twilight, when the lights are low,
And the flick'ring shadows softly come and go,
Tho' the heart be weary, sad the day and long,
Still to us at twilight comes Love's old song,
comes Love's old sweet song.

Even today we hear Love's song of yore,
Deep in our hearts it dwells forevermore.
Footsteps may falter, weary grow the way,
Still we can hear it at the close of day.

So till the end, when life's dim shadows fall,
Love will be found the sweetest song of all.
Just a song a twilight, when the lights are low,
And the flick'ring shadows softly come and go,
Tho' the heart be weary, sad the day and long,
Still to us at twilight comes Love's old song,
comes Love's old sweet song.

---

① 作为典故,此歌谣出现于《尤利西斯》,其作者为格雷厄姆·克利夫顿·宾厄姆(Graham Clifton Bingham, 1859—1913)。

| 乔伊斯作品中的
凯尔特歌谣

爱人那动听的老歌

在那回忆业已朦胧的久远时期，
当时，大地上开始弥漫重重薄雾，
欢情从一系列梦中涌出
爱人唱过一首动听老歌在我们心头响起；
伴随薄暮中的炉火闪烁，
它悄然潜入我们的梦境。

当灯光暗淡，恰逢黄昏，传来一首歌，
那昔日的系列情景在悄然闪动，
虽然内心疲惫，白天伤感而漫长，
黄昏时爱人的老歌依然向我们传来，
传来爱人那动听的老歌。

甚至到今天，我们仍听到爱人昔日唱过的歌，
它永远萦回于我们心中。
脚步会蹒跚，路上会疲惫，
日落时分，我们仍能听到它。

就这样，直到生命投下暗影，
所有歌中，唯有情歌最觉动听。
当灯光暗淡，恰逢黄昏，传来一首歌，
那昔日的系列情景在悄然闪动，
虽然内心疲惫，白天伤感而漫长，
黄昏时爱人的老歌依然向我们传来，
传来爱人那动听的老歌。

Those Lovely Seaside Girls[①]

Down at Margate looking very charming you are sure to meet
Those girls, dear girls, those lovely seaside girls.
With sticks they steer and promenade the pier to give the boys a treat;
In piqué silks and lace, they tip you quite a playful wink.
It always is the case: you seldom stop to think.
You fall in love of course upon the spot,
But not with one girl — always with the lot ...
Those girls, those girls, those lovely seaside girls,
All dimples, smiles, and curls — your head it simply whirls!
They look all right, complexions pink and white;
They've diamond rings and dainty feet,
Golden hair from Regent Street,
Lace and grace and lots of face — those pretty little seaside girls.

There's Maud and Clara, Gwendoline and Sarah — where do they come from?
Those girls, dear girls, those lovely seaside girls.
In bloomers smart they captivate the heart when cycling down the prom;
At wheels and heels and hose you must not look, 'tis understood,
But every Johnnie knows: it does the eyesight good.
The boys observe the latest thing in socks;
They learn the time — by looking at the clocks ...
Those girls, those girls, those lovely seaside girls,
All dimples, smiles, and curls — your head it simply whirls!
They look all right, complexions pink and white;
They've diamond rings and dainty feet,

---

① 作为典故,此歌谣出现于《尤利西斯》,其作者为 H. B. 诺里斯(H. B. Norris)。

那些可爱的海滨姑娘

从马盖特望去，景色很迷人。你肯定会遇到
那些姑娘，亲爱的姑娘们，那些可爱的海滨姑娘。
她们持桨划船，并在码头散步，款待小伙儿们；
她们身着丝绸和蕾丝衣，顽皮地向你眨一下眼。
情况总如此，你几乎不假思索。
你当然会当场坠入爱河，
但不是爱上一个姑娘——总会爱上多个……
那些姑娘，那些姑娘，那些可爱的海滨姑娘，
那些酒窝，那些微笑，那些卷发——简直会让你神魂颠倒！
她们长相端正，肤色白皙粉嫩；
她们手戴钻戒，玉足纤纤，
长着摄政街特有的金发，
蕾丝、优雅，笑靥朵朵——那些漂亮的海滨小姑娘。

姑娘们有莫德、克拉拉、格温德琳和莎拉——她们来自哪里？
那些姑娘，亲爱的姑娘们，那些可爱的海滨姑娘。
她们身着时髦的灯笼裤，在毕业舞会飞旋起舞偷心无数；
你切莫瞅裙撑、脚跟和长筒袜，不言而喻，
但是每个男孩都知道：这的确赏心悦目。
男孩们从袜子上观察最新潮流；
正如他们得知时间——靠看看钟表……
那些姑娘，那些姑娘，那些可爱的海滨姑娘，
那些酒窝，那些微笑，那些卷发——简直会让你神魂颠倒！
她们长相端正，肤色白皙粉嫩；
她们手戴钻戒，玉足纤纤，

Golden hair from Regent Street,

Lace and grace and lots of face — those pretty little seaside girls.

When you go to do a little boating, just for fun you take

Those girls, dear girls, those lovely seaside girls.

They all say, "We so dearly love the sea!" Their way on board they make;

The wind begins to blow: each girl remarks, "How rough today!"

"It's lovely, don't you know!" — and then they sneak away.

And as the yacht keeps rolling with the tide,

You'll notice, hanging o'er the vessel's side . . .

Those girls, those girls, those lovely seaside girls,

All dimples, smiles, and curls — your head it simply whirls!

They look a sight, complexions GREEN and white;

Their hats fly off, and at your feet

Falls golden hair from Regent Street,

Rouge and puffs slip down the cuffs — of pretty little seaside girls.

长着摄政街特有的金发，

蕾丝、优雅——那些漂亮的海滨小姑娘。

当你去划划船，只是图个乐子而带着

那些姑娘，亲爱的姑娘们，那些可爱的海滨姑娘。

她们都说："我们非常喜欢大海！"她们在船上走来走去；

风开始吹：每个女孩都在议论："今天天气真糟！"

"天气挺好，你不知道而已！"——然后，她们就偷偷溜走。

当游艇随着潮水不断打转，

你将注意到，正依靠船舷的……

那些姑娘，那些姑娘，那些可爱的海滨姑娘，

那些酒窝，那些微笑和卷发——简直会让你神魂颠倒！

她们看起来娇美如画，皮肤鲜嫩而白皙；

她们抛出一顶顶帽子，扔到你脚旁

垂下摄政街特有的金发，

胭脂和粉扑滑出——漂亮的海滨小姑娘的袖口。

My Girl's a Yorkshire Girl[①]

Two young fellows were talking about
Their girls, girls, girls —
Sweethearts they'd left behind,
Sweethearts for whom they pined.
One said, "My little shy little lass
Has a waist so trim and small.
Gray are her eyes so bright,
But best, best of all ...

"My girl's a Yorkshire girl —
Yorkshire through and through.
My girl's a Yorkshire girl,
Eh! by gum, she's a champion!
Though she's a factory lass
And wears no fancy clothes,
Still I've a sort of a Yorkshire relish
For my little Yorkshire Rose."

When the first finished singing the praise
Of Rose, Rose, Rose,
Poor number two looked vexed,
Saying in tones perplexed：
"My lass works in a factory too
And has also eyes of gray；
Her name is Rose as well,

---

① 作为典故，此歌谣出现于《尤利西斯》，其作者为查尔斯·威廉·墨菲（Charles William Murphy，1870—1913）及达恩·利普顿（Dan Lipton，1873—1935）。

我女友是约克郡女孩

两个年轻小伙曾谈论着
他们的女友们，女友们，女友们——
他们永远离开的恋人们，
他们怀恋的恋人们。
一人说："我那腼腆而可爱的小女孩
腰部苗条又小巧。
她的双眼灰又亮，
但她最好，是所有人中最好的……

"我女友是约克郡女孩——
地地道道的约克郡人。
我女友是约克郡女孩，
啊！天哪，她最棒了！
她虽是工厂女工
穿的也不华丽，
我仍对约克郡情有独钟
为了我的约克郡小玫瑰。"

第一个小伙唱完
玫瑰、玫瑰、玫瑰的赞歌，
可怜的第二个小伙则显露烦恼，
不解地说道：
"我女友也在工厂上班
也长一双灰色眼睛；
她名字也是玫瑰，

And strange, strange to say ...

"My girl's a Yorkshire girl —
Yorkshire through and through.
My girl's a Yorkshire girl,
Eh! by gum, she's a champion!
Though she's a factory lass
And wears no fancy clothes,
Still I've a sort of a Yorkshire relish
For my little Yorkshire Rose."

To a cottage in Yorkshire they hied
To Rose, Rose, Rose,
Meaning to make it clear
Which was the boy most dear.
Rose, their Rose, didn't answer the bell,
But her husband did instead.
Loudly he sang to them
As off, off they fled ...

"My girl's a Yorkshire girl —
Yorkshire through and through.
My girl's a Yorkshire girl,
Eh! by gum, she's a champion!
Though she's a factory lass
And wears no fancy clothes,
Still I've a sort of a Yorkshire relish
For my little Yorkshire Rose."

乔伊斯作品中的
凯 尔 特 歌 谣

并且,不自在、不自在地说……

"我女友是约克郡女孩——
地地道道的约克郡人。
我女友是约克郡女孩,
啊！天哪,她最棒了！
她虽是工厂女工
穿的也不华丽,
我仍对约克郡情有独钟
为了我的约克郡小玫瑰。"

他们赶紧去约克郡的一间小屋
找玫瑰、玫瑰、玫瑰,
想弄清楚
哪个小伙她最爱。
玫瑰、他们的玫瑰并不开门迎客,
而她丈夫则代劳。
他冲他们大声吼
他们则逃之夭夭……

"我女友是约克郡女孩——
地地道道的约克郡人。
我女友是约克郡女孩,
啊！天哪,她最棒了！
她虽是工厂女工
穿的也不华丽,
我仍对约克郡情有独钟
为了我的约克郡小玫瑰。"

The Holy City[①]

Last night I lay a-sleeping
There came a dream so fair，
I stood in old Jerusalem
Beside the temple there.
I heard the children singing，
And ever as they sang
Methought the voice of angels
From heaven in answer rang.
Methought the voice of angels
From heaven in answer rang.

Jerusalem! Jerusalem!
Lift up your gates and sing，
Hosanna in the highest!
Hosanna to your King!

And then methought my dream was
changed，
The streets no longer rang.
Hushed were the glad Hosannas
The little children sang.
The sun grew dark with mystery，
The morn was cold and chill，
As the shadow of a cross arose
Upon a lonely hill，

---

① 作为典故，此歌谣出现于《斯蒂芬英雄》和《尤利西斯》，其作者为弗雷德里克·爱德华·韦瑟利(Frederic Edward Weatherly, 1848—1929)。

圣城

昨夜，我平卧而眠

做了一个好梦，

我站在耶路撒冷古城

在那里的神殿旁。

我听到孩子们在歌唱，

每当他们唱歌时

我认为来自天国众天使之声

在回响。

我以为来自天国众天使之声

在回响。

耶路撒冷！耶路撒冷！

升起你那一道道大门而歌唱，

至高的赞美！

赞美归于你的王！

然后，我认为我的梦境变了，

那些街道不再有回声。

那群小孩们欢快唱出

的赞美之声沉寂了。

阳光神秘兮兮地逐渐黯淡，

早晨阴沉而寒冷，

当时，一副十字架的影子

在一座荒山上延伸，

As the shadow of a cross arose
Upon a lonely hill.

Jerusalem! Jerusalem!
Hark! How the angels sing,
Hosanna in the highest!
Hosanna to your King!

And once again the scene was changed,
New earth there seemed to be.
I saw the Holy City
Beside the tideless sea.
The light of God was on its streets,
The gates were open wide,
And all who would might enter,
And no one was denied.
No need of moon or stars by night,
Or sun to shine by day;
It was the new Jerusalem
That would not pass away,
It was the new Jerusalem
That would not pass away.

Jerusalem! Jerusalem!
Sing for the night is o'er!
Hosanna in the highest!
Hosanna forevermore!

(As an allusion, this song appears in *Stephen Hero* and *Ulysses*.)

当时，一副十字架的影子
在一座荒山上延伸。

耶路撒冷！耶路撒冷！
听！众天使竟这样唱歌，
至高的赞美！
赞美归于你的王！

场景再一次改变，
似乎出现新世界。
我曾见圣城
坐落于风平浪静的海边。
上帝之光映照圣城的一道道大街，
一堵堵城门敞开，
所有想进城的人中，
无一人受阻。
夜间无需月亮与群星，
昼间亦无需太阳照耀；
这是崭新的耶路撒冷
它不会消失，
这是崭新的耶路撒冷
它不会消失。

耶路撒冷！耶路撒冷！
夜已过去，为此唱吧！
至高的赞美！
永恒的赞美！

M'appari(or, "Martha, Martha, O Return Love!")①

From the Opera *Martha*

When first I saw that form endearing,

Sorrow from me seem'd to depart：

Each graceful look，each word so cheering，

Charm'd my eye and won my heart.

Full of hope，and all delighted，

None could feel more blest than I；

All on earth I then could wish for，

Was near her to live and die：

But alas! 'twas idle dreaming，

And the dream too soon hath flown；

Not one ray of hope is gleaming；

I am lost，yes I am lost，for she is gone.

When first I saw that form endearing,

Sorrow from me seem'd to depart：

Each graceful look，each word so cheering，

Charm'd my eye and won my heart.

Martha，Martha，I am sighing，

I am weeping still，for thee；

Come thou lost one，Come though dear one，

---

① 作为典故，此歌谣出现于《尤利西斯》和《为芬尼根守灵》，原德国歌剧，该英文版本由查尔斯·
杰弗里斯(Charles Jeffreys，1807—1865)翻译而成。

恍若一梦("玛莎,玛莎,哦,回来吧,我的爱人!")

——歌剧《玛莎》片段

当我初次看见那迷人身材,
忧伤似乎离我而去:
每个优雅的表情、每句令人振奋的话语,
都吸引我的目光,并赢得我的心。

充满希望,满心欢喜,
没人比我更幸运;
于是,我在这世上所能企求的,
就是在她身边生与死:

但是,唉!这是白日梦,
而此梦转瞬即破灭;
没有闪出一线希望之光;
我一筹莫展,对,我一筹莫展,因为她走了。

当初次看见那迷人身材,
忧伤似乎离我而去:
每个优雅的表情、每句令人振奋的话语,
都吸引我的目光,并赢得我的心。

玛莎,玛莎,我在叹息,
我仍在哭泣,就为你;
迷惘的人,你来吧,亲爱的人,你来吧,

Thou alone can'st comfort me:

Ah! Martha return! Come to me!

只有你才让我感到宽慰：

啊！玛莎回来吧！来到我身边吧！

The Bloom Is on the Rye (or, "My Pretty Jane")①

My pretty Jane! My pretty Jane!

Ah! Never, never look so shy.

But meet me, meet me in the Ev'ning,

While the bloom is on the Rye.

The Spring is waning fast, my love,

The corn is in the ear.

The Summer nights are coming, Love,

The moon shines bright and clear;

Then pretty Jane, my dearest Jane,

Ah! never look so shy,

But meet me, meet me in the Ev'ning,

While the bloom is on the Rye.

But name the day, the wedding day,

And I will buy the ring,

The Lads and Maids in favours while,

And village bells, the village bells shall ring.

The Spring is waning fast, my love,

The corn is in the ear.

The Summer nights are coming, Love,

The moon shines bright and clear;

Then pretty Jane, my dearest Jane,

Ah! never look so shy,

But meet me, meet me in the Ev'ning,

While the bloom is on the Rye.

---

① 作为典故,此歌谣出现于《尤利西斯》,其作者为爱德华·菲茨伯尔(Edward Fitzball, 1792—1873)。

| 乔伊斯作品中的
凯 尔 特 歌 谣

小穗缀黑麦之季(或"我俊俏的简")

我俊俏的简！我俊俏的简！
啊！从未，从未显得如此害羞。
但是，遇见我，遇见我的那晚，
正值小穗缀黑麦之季。
春天即将过去，我的爱人，
谷物正在抽穗。
一个个夏夜就要来临，爱人啊，
月儿明又圆；
嗯，俊俏的简，我最亲爱的简，
啊！从未显得如此害羞，
但是，遇见我，遇见我的那晚，
正值小穗缀黑麦之季。

要不就定下日子，婚礼之日，
然后，我将购买婚戒，
小伙们和少女们来捧场，
而一座座乡村的、一座座乡村的钟会敲响。
春天即将过去，我的爱人，
谷物正在抽穗。
一个个夏夜就要来临，爱人啊，
月儿明又圆；
嗯，俊俏的简，我最亲爱的简，
啊！从未显得如此害羞，
但是，遇见我，遇见我的那晚，
正值小穗缀黑麦之季。

The Low-back'd Car[①]

When first I saw sweet Peggy,
'Twas on a market day;
A low-back'd car she drove, and sat
Upon a truss of hay;
But when that hay was blooming grass,
And deck'd with flowers of Spring,
No flow'r was there that could compare
With the blooming girl I sing.

  As she sat in the low-back'd car,
  The man at the turnpike bar
  Never ask'd for the toll,
  But just rubb'd his owld poll
  And looked after the low-backed car.

In battle's wild commotion,
The proud and mighty Mars
With hostile scythes demands his tithes
Of death — in warlike cars;
While Peggy, peaceful goddess,
Has darts in her bright eye
That knock men down, in the market-town,
As right and left they fly;

  While she sits in the low-back'd car,

---

① 作为典故,此歌谣出现于《尤利西斯》和《为芬尼根守灵》,其作者为塞缪尔·洛弗(Samuel Lover, 1797—1868)。

矮背四轮马车

我初见可爱的佩姬之时，
是在一个集市日；
她驾一辆矮背四轮马车，并坐在
一捆干草垛上；
但当干草尚为茂盛的青草，
并缀以春天花朵时，
没有一朵花能媲美
我赞颂的风华正茂的姑娘。

当她坐在那辆矮背四轮马车上，
收费关卡的那个男人
从不索要过路费，
而仅仅揉着他手中的旧登记册
且目送那辆矮背四轮马车。

在战场上那失控的骚动中，
那骄傲而强大的战神
在一辆辆战车上
用敌人的长柄大镰刀，为其征收死亡什一税；
而佩姬，身为和平女神，
她发亮的目光中有一支支飞镖
在那座集镇，飞镖将一个又一个男人击倒，
当时他们东奔西逃；

当她坐在那辆矮背四轮马车上，

Than battle more dangerous far —
For the doctor's art,
Cannot cure the heart
That is hit from that low-back'd car.

Sweet Peggy round her car, sir
Has strings of ducks and geese,
But the scores of hearts she slaughters
By far outnumber these;
While she among her poultry sits,
Just like a turtle-dove,
Well worth the cage, I do engage,
　Of the blooming god of love;

　While she sits in her low-back'd car,
　The lovers come near and far,
　And envy the chicken
　That Peggy is pickin',
　As she sits in her low-back'd car.

Oh, I'd rather own that car, sir,
With Peggy by my side,
Than a coach-and-four, and gold galore,
And a lady for my bride;
For the lady would sit forninst me,
On a cushion made with taste,
While Peggy would sit beside me,
With my arm around her waist,

　While we drove in the low-back'd car
　To be married by Father Maher;

战斗愈加险恶——
以大夫的医技，
无法治疗被那辆矮背四轮马车
打击过的内心。

先生，可爱的佩姬在其车旁
有一群群鸭和鹅，
但是她所伤害的心灵
在数目上远超鸭鹅的量；
她坐在家禽中，
恰似一只斑鸠，
我保证，她很配，
　　有旺盛精力的爱神之笼；

　　当她坐在其矮背四轮马车上，
　　爱慕者们来自四面八方，
　　忌妒那只
　　佩姬坐在其矮背四轮马车上，
　　所选中的鸡。

哦，先生，我多想拥有那辆马车，
由佩姬陪在我身旁，
有一位女士做我的新娘，
胜过拥有一辆四轮马车和黄金万两；
因为这位女士愿优雅地垫着软垫，
坐在我身旁，
当佩姬愿坐在我身旁，
她的腰被我单手搂抱，

　　当我们驾驶那辆矮背四轮马车
　　由马厄神父主婚；

Oh，my heart would beat high
At her glance and her sigh，
Though it beat in a low-back'd car.

|

哦，为她的一瞥和一叹
我的心会狂跳，
尽管在一辆矮背四轮马车上怦然心动。

The Croppy Boy[1]

"Good men and true in this house who dwell,
To a stranger bouchal[2] I pray you tell:
Is the priest at home, or may he be seen?
I would speak a word with Father Green."

"The Priest's at home, boy, and may be seen;
'Tis easy speaking with Father Green.
But you must wait till I go and see
If the Holy Father alone may be."
The youth has enter'd an empty hall;
What a lonely sound has his light footfall!
And the gloomy chamber's chill and bare,
With a vested Priest in a lonely chair.

The youth has knelt to tell his sins:
"Nomine Dei," the youth begins!
At "mea culpa" he beats his breast,
And in brokenmurmers he speaks the rest.

"At the siege of Ross did my father fall,
And at Gorey my loving brothers all.
I alone am left of my name and race;
I will go to Wexford and take their place.

"I cursed three times since last Easter day;

---

① 作为典故,此歌谣出现于《尤利西斯》,其作者为卡洛尔·马隆(Carrol Malone,1844—1892)。
② 爱尔兰语,意为"男孩;小伙儿"。

那推平头的小伙

"居于此屋中善良而正直的人们，
我请求你们告诉一个外来小伙：
神父是否在家，或能见见他吗？
我想与格林神父说句话。"

"孩子啊，神父在呢，而且，可以见他；
与格林神父交谈并不难。
但你得等我去看看
是不是神父身边没人。"
那位青年已走进空旷礼堂；
他那轻快的脚步发出一个多么孤单的响声！
阴暗的房间冷飕飕而光秃秃，
惟有一位身着圣衣的牧师孤零零地坐在椅子上。

那位青年已跪下讲述他的一些罪过：
那位青年开口道："以上帝之名！"
他捶胸说，"是我的错"，
并断断续续地诉说剩余的话语。

"我父亲在围攻罗斯时阵亡，
我那富有爱心的兄弟们都死在戈里。
在我的姓氏和种族中，仅剩我一人；
我会去韦克斯福德夺取他们的地点。

"自去年复活节以来，我三次咒骂；

At mass time once I went to play;
I passed the churchyard one day in haste,
And forgot to pray for my mother's rest.

"I bear no hate against living thing,
But I love my country above my King.
Now, Father! bless me and let me go
To die, if God has ordained it so."

The Priest said nought, but a rustling noise
Made the youth look above in wild surprise;
The robes were off, and in scarlet there
Sat a yeoman captain with a fiery glare.

With fiery glare and with fury hoarse,
Instead of blessing, he breathed a curse:
"'Twas a good thought, boy, to come here and shrive,
for one short hour is your time to live.

"Upon yon river three tenders float;
The Priest's in one —— if he isn't shot!
We hold his house for our Lord and King,
And, amen say I, may all traitors swing!"

At Geneva Barrack that young man died,
And at Passage①they have his body laid.
Good people who live in peace and joy,
Breathe a pray'r and a tear for the Croppy Boy.

---

① "Passage"(帕西奇)亦作"Passage West"(西帕西奇)位于爱尔兰克科郡的一个港口镇,它的爱
尔兰名称为"An Pasáiste Thiar"。

有一次，在弥撒时间，我去玩耍；
一天，我匆忙经过教堂墓地，
忘记为我母亲的安息而祈祷。

"我并不厌恶生物，
只是我爱我国胜过我王。
哎，神父！祝福我，让我去吧
去死，若这是上帝的旨意。"

那位神父不语，但发出窸窣声
使那位青年愕然举目；
层层长袍被脱，一袭红衣露出
一位目光炯炯的义勇骑兵队队长坐在那儿。

他的目光如炬，发出狂怒的嘶哑声，
非但不予祝福：而张口诅咒道：
"小子，来这忏悔是个好主意，
因为你只能再活短短一小时了。

"那条河面上漂浮着三条船；
那位神父若没被击毙——会在一条船里！
为了我们的主和王，我们占有他的房屋，
我说，愿叛徒们都被绞死，阿门！"

那位青年死于日内瓦兵营，
他们把他的尸体葬于帕西奇。
在和平与快乐中生活的良民们，
为推平头的小伙祈祷和落泪。

In the Shade of the Palm[①]

There is a garden fair, set in an Eastern sea.

There is a maid keeping her tryst with me.

In the shade of the palm, with a lover's delight,

Where 'tis ever the golden day, or a silvery night.

How can I leave her along in this dream of sweet Arcadia?

How can I part from her for lands away?

In this valley of Eden, fairest isle of the sea,

Oh, my beloved, bid me to stay! In this fair land of Eden,

Bid me, belov'd to stay!

CHORUS:

Oh, my Dolores, Queen of the Eastern sea!

Fair one of Eden, look to the West for me!

My star will be shining, love, when you're in the moonlight calm,

So be waiting for me by the Eastern sea,

In the shade of the shelt'ring palm!

There is an island fair, girt by a Western sea,

Dearest, 'tis there one day thou'lt go with me.

Neath the glorious moon hand in hand we will roam,

Hear the nightingale sing in June, in the dear land of Home!

There, dearest heart, will the past but seem an idle vision,

Naught but a dream that fadeth fast away,

---

① 作为典故,此歌谣出现于《尤利西斯》,其作者为莱斯利·斯图尔特(Leslie Stuart, 1863—
1928)。

在那棕榈树荫下

有座美丽的花园,以东海为背景。
有位少女与我保持着恋情。
在那棕榈树荫下,怀着恋人的欣喜,
在那里,白天阳光灿烂,夜晚月光如银。
我怎能把她落在可爱的阿卡迪亚这样的理想圣地?
我怎能把她落在遥远的地方?
在海上最美的小岛上,这道伊甸山谷里,
哦,我的爱人,莫让我走! 在此美丽的伊甸园,
亲爱的,莫让我走!

副歌:
哦,我的多洛雷丝,东海女王!
伊甸园中的美人,为我留意西方!
爱人啊,你在无风的月光下时,我的幸运之星会闪闪发亮,
因而,在东海之滨等着我吧,
就在那棕榈树荫下!

有座美丽的岛,被西海环绕,
最亲爱的,总有一天,你会伴随我。
在宜人的月光下,我们将牵手漫步,
六月里听夜莺在亲爱的家乡土地上啼啭!
亲爱的心肝,在那里,往事将仅仅像一个无意义的幻觉,
除了像一场倏然而逝的梦,它一无是处,

And the songs we were singing in Elysian vales，

Seem but a carol of yesterday! Happy songs we were singing,

Songs of a bygone day!

我们在极乐世界一道道溪谷中唱的一首首歌，
似乎仅为昨日颂歌！我们曾唱着一首首快乐的歌，
一首首往日之歌！

My Lady's Bower[①]

Thro' the moated grange at twilight, my love and I we went,
By empty rooms and lonely stairs, in lover's sweet content,
And round the old and broken casement, we watched the roses flow'r,
But the place we lov'd the best of all, was call'd "My Lady's Bow'r."

And with beating hearts we enter'd and stood and whisper'd low,
Of the sweet and lovely lady who liv'd there years ago!
And the moon shone in upon us across the dusty floor,
Where her little feet had wandered in the courtly days of yore;
And it touch'd the faded arras and again we seem'd to see
The lovely lady sitting there, her lover at her knee,
And we saw him kiss her fair white hand and Oh! we heard him say:
"I shall love thee love for ever, Tho' the years may pass away!
I shall love thee, for ever! Tho' the years may pass away!"

But then they vanish'd in a moment, and we knew 'twas but a dream!
It was not they who sat there in the sliver moonlight gleam!
Ah! no, 'twas we, we two together who had found our golden hour,
And told the old, old story within "My Lady's Bow'r,"
And told the old, old story within "My Lady's Bow'r."

---

① 作为典故,此歌谣出现于《尤利西斯》,其作者为弗雷德里克·爱德华·韦瑟利(Frederic Edward Weatherly, 1848—1929)。

吾妻亭

黄昏，我和爱人穿过那座壕沟环绕的庄园，

经过一间间空房，踏过一片片人迹罕至的台阶，令爱人愉快而满足，

在破旧窗户四周，我们欣赏了一朵朵玫瑰花，

而我们最钟爱之处则被叫做"吾妻亭"。

在怦然心动中，我们步入，驻足，悄声低语，

谈及多年前居住于此的那位迷人而可爱的夫人！

当时，月光照在我们身上，洒在布满灰尘的地上，

在昔日宫廷时期，她移动小足，徘徊于此；

月光映照于褪色的挂毯，而我们似乎又见

那位可爱的夫人坐在那里，由她爱人陪在膝旁，

而我们目睹他亲吻她一只美丽的素手，哦！我们听他说：

"虽然岁月会流逝，我一定永远爱你！

虽然岁月会流逝，我一定永远爱你！"

但是，随后他们一下子便突然消失了，而我们则意识到这只是一场梦！

在朦胧的银色月光下坐在那儿的并不是他们！

啊！不是他们，而是我们，我俩发现了我们的美好时刻，

而在"吾妻亭"，讲述那则古老的、古老的故事，

而在"吾妻亭"，讲述那则古老的、古老的故事。

What-Ho! She Bumps! [①]

I've been out on a pleasure boat for a day on the breezy brine;

We started away from London Bridge, and we all felt fit and fine,

We sang "A Life on the Ocean Wave" [②] as loud as we could roar,

Our boat went alright down the Thames, but when we reached the Nore [③]—

She began to bump a little bit, bump, bump, bump, just a little bit;

A fat man fell down the engine room, his wife was clinging to the great jibboom,

She roll'd about, and, fairly in the dumps, I clung to the Captain's bags, and cried:

"What-ho! she bumps!"

I once played in a drama that we called "The Flying Scud,

I'd to appear on a gee-gee, and it was a bit of blood!

In front of the blooming audience I had to mount her nibs,

And when I stuck a pin into her india rubber ribs —

She began to bump a little bit, bump, bump, bump, just a little bit;

Oh, she made a tremendous hit when she kick'd our villain in the threep'ny bit;

The actors guyed as she took running jumps,

And a boy in the gallery cried, Encore, "What-ho! she bumps!"

Where I lived at the seaside once a girl lived opposite,

And one fine morning she went to bathe in a costume pink and white;

A crowd of chaps stood on the shore as she waded in the blue,

---

① 作为典故,此歌谣出现于《尤利西斯》,其作者为哈里·卡斯林(Harry Castling, 1865—1933)。

② A Life on the Ocean Wave 是由埃佩斯·萨金特(Epes Sargent)创作的一首诗歌,出版于 1838 年,由亨利·罗素(Henry Russell)谱曲。

③ 诺尔(英泰晤士河一沙岛)。

嘿！船晃了！

在微风吹拂的海面，我外出乘游艇玩了一天；
我们从伦敦桥起航，都感觉健康又快乐，
当时，我们尽兴高唱一曲《海浪上的生活》，
我们的船已沿泰晤士河而下，但当我们抵达诺尔——
船开始有点晃，砰、砰、砰，只有一点晃；
一个胖子从机舱摔下，他的妻子则抓紧那根巨大的第二斜桅，
船来回摇，也相当晃，我抓紧船长的那些旅行袋，并大叫：
"嘿！船晃了！"

我演过一部戏，我们把该戏叫作"行云"，
我应在马儿的背上露个面儿，而它是一种小惩罚！
在狂热的观众前，我不得不骑上这匹自命不凡的母马，
而当我把一根别针插入母马那胶皮肋骨之间时——
母马开始有点晃，砰、砰、砰，只有一点晃；
哦，母马踢了三便士硬币中我们的反派主角，它就大出风头；
当母马边跑边跳时，那些演员便勒紧缰绳，
楼座的男孩喊道，再来一个，"嘿！母马晃了！"

我曾住在海边，一个女孩就住对面，
在一个晴朗的上午，她身着粉白相间的泳衣，出门去戏水；
当她在蓝色大海中蹚水时，一群小伙儿则在岸上站着，

And ev'ryone was, anxious there to see what she would do.

She began to bump a little bit, bump, bump, bump, just a little bit;

At first she was bashful as she could be, till she got used to the rolling sea,

Then up and down the little petlet jumps,

and the men all shouted from the golden shore: "What-ho! she bumps!"

在那儿，人人都渴望看看她要干什么。
她开始有点晃，砰、砰、砰，只有一点晃；
她最初极为忸怩，直到她适应了起伏的海浪，
接着，这个小宝贝儿跳来跳去，
而那些男人都在金色水岸喊道："嘿！她晃了！"

Shall I Wear a White Rose?[①]

Shall I wear a white rose, shall I wear a red?

Will he look for garlands? What shall wreathe my head?

Will a riband charm him fair upon my breast?

Scarce I can remember how he loves me best.

Shall I wear a white rose, shall I wear a red?

Will he look for garlands? What shall wreathe my head?

I must look my fairest when tomorrow's here;

He will come to claim me! Shall I still be dear?

I must look my brightest on that happy day,

As his fancy drew me when so far away,

When so far away.

I shall need no roses if his heart be true

Not a single wreathlet, red or white or blue.

In tomorrow's twilight, when my soul's at rest,

Then I need not ask him how he loves me best.

Shall I wear a white rose, shall I wear a red?

Will he look for garlands? What shall wreathe my head?

---

① 作为典故,此歌谣出现于《尤利西斯》,其作者为亨利·萨维尔·克拉克(Henry Savile Clarke, 1841—1893)。

| 乔伊斯作品中的
凯 尔 特 歌 谣

我要不要戴朵白玫瑰?

我要不要戴朵白玫瑰,我要不要戴朵红的?
他会不会对一些花环有所期待? 我头上该戴什么花环?
我胸前的缎带会不会让他很着迷?
我几乎忘记他如何尽可能地爱我。
我要不要戴朵白玫瑰,我要不要戴朵红的?
他会不会对一些花环有所期待? 我头上该戴什么花环?

到了明天,我定要显出我最美的样子;
他会来向我表白! 我还是宝贝儿吗?
在那幸福之日,我定要显得光彩之至,
因为他曾中意于我在那很遥远的过去,
在那很遥远的过去。

若他有真心,我就不要任何玫瑰
连个花环也不要,不管它是红的、白的,还是蓝的。
明天黄昏,在我的心定下来时,
到那时,我不需要问他会怎样尽力爱我。
我要不要戴朵白玫瑰,我要不要戴朵红的?
他会不会对一些花环有所期待? 我头上该戴什么花环?

In Old Madrid[①]

Long years ago, in old Madrid,

Where softly sighs of love the light guitar,

Two sparkling eyes a lattice hid,

Two eyes as darkly bright as love's own star!

There on the casement ledge when day was o'er,

A tiny hand was lightly laid;

A face look'd out, as from the river shore,

There stole a tender serenade!

Rang the lover's happy song

Light and low from shore to shore,

But ah! the river flow'd along

Between them evermore!

CHORUS:

Come, my love, the stars are shining,

Time is flying,

Love is sighing,

Come, for thee a heart is pining,

Here alone I wait for thee!

Far, far away from old Madrid,

Her lover fell, long years ago, for Spain;

A convent veil those sweet eyes hid;

And all the vows that love had sigh'd were vain!

But still, between the dusk and night, 'tis said,

---

① 作为典故,此歌谣出现于《尤利西斯》,其作者为格雷厄姆·克利夫顿·宾厄姆(Graham Clifton Bingham,1859—1913)。

乔伊斯作品中的
凯 尔 特 歌 谣

在古老的马德里

多年前，在古老的马德里，
那里有一声声爱的微叹和轻弹的吉他，
窗格后藏着一双亮晶晶的眼睛，
那双眼如爱神那独特之星乌黑又闪亮！
白天将尽时，在窗上，
轻搭着一只小小的手；
一张脸向外张望，当时从河岸，
悄悄传来一只柔和的小夜曲！
爱人的欢歌
于两岸悠扬地回响，
然而，啊！河水沿着两岸
永无止息地流动！

副歌：
来吧，我的爱人，群星在闪烁，
时光在飞逝，
爱神在叹息，
来吧，一颗心在为你痛苦，
在此，我只为等候你！

距古老的马德里很远，很远，
为了西班牙，她爱人于多年前战死；
那双迷人的眼睛藏在一张修女面纱下；
而爱人所言的所有誓言都付之东流！
但是，在暮与夜之交，据说，

Her white hand opes the lattice wide，
The faint sweet echo of that serenade，
Floats weirdly o'er the misty tide!
Still she lists her lover's song，
Still he sings upon the shore，
Though flows a stream than all more strong
Between them evermore!

她那白皙的手依然敞开窗格，
小夜曲那依稀可闻的悦耳回声，
不可思议地飘荡于薄雾弥漫潮面！
她依然喜欢她爱人的歌，
他依然在岸上演唱，
尽管一条小溪沿着两岸更加汹涌
永无止息地流动！

The Lost Chord[①]

Seated one day at the organ, I was weary and ill at ease,
And my fingers wander'd idly over the noisy keys;
I knew not what I was playing, or what I was dreaming then,
But I struck one chord of music like the sound of a great Amen.

It flooded the crimson twilight like the close of an Angel's Psalm,
And it lay on my fever'd spirit with a touch of infinite calm.
It quieted pain and sorrow like love overcoming strife,
It seem'd the harmonious echo from our discordant life.

It link'd all perplexed meanings into one perfect peace
And trembled away into silence as if it were loth to cease;
I have sought, but I seek it vainly, that one lost chord divine,
Which came from the soul of the organ and enter'd into mine.

It may be that Death's bright Angel will speak in that chord again;
It may be that only in Heav'n I shall hear that grand Amen!

---

① 作为典故，此歌谣出现于《尤利西斯》，其作者为雅德蕾德·安妮·普罗克特（Adelaide Anne Procter，1825—1864）。

失落的和弦

一天,我坐在管风琴前,疲倦又不安,
我的这些手指懒散地来回敲击在那些含噪音的琴键上;
我当时不知道自己在弹奏什么,也不清楚自己正想象什么,
但我弹奏了一个像美妙的《阿门曲》中的和弦音。

它像一首天使赞美诗的结尾,洋溢于深红色的暮光中,
而且,它以一丝极度平静,笼罩着我那焦虑的心灵。
它像爱意战胜冲突那样,平息了痛苦和悲伤,
它似乎源自我们那矛盾生活的和谐回音。

它把所有令人迷惑的含义,并入一份安宁
而后,它仿佛不情愿终止,颤动着消失于沉默之中;
我寻找过那一失落的绝妙和弦,但徒劳无获,
那和弦来自管风琴的感染力,并融入我的灵魂。

或许,死神的光明天使又将在此和弦中说话;
或许,只有在天堂,我才会听到那首美妙的《阿门曲》!

The Boys of Wexford[①]

In comes the captain's daughter,
The captain of the Yeos,
Saying "Brave United Irishmen,
We'll ne'er again be foes.
A thousand pounds I'll bring
If you will fly from home with me,
And dress myself in man's attire
And fight for liberty."

We are the boys of Wexford,
Who fouht with heart and hand
To burst in twain the galling chain
And free our native land.

I want no gold, my maiden fair,
To fly from home with thee.
Your shining eyes will be my prize,
More dear than gold to me.
I want no gold to nerve my arm
To do a true man's part —
To free my land I'd gladly give
The red drops of my heart ... chorus

And when we left our cabins, boys,
We left with right good will

---

① 作为典故,此歌谣出现于《尤利西斯》和《为芬尼根守灵》,其作者为帕特里克·约瑟夫·麦考尔(Patrick Joseph McCall, 1861—1919)。

韦克斯福德的男小伙儿们

上尉的女儿进来，
是义勇骑兵上尉的女儿，
说着"爱尔兰联合会的勇士们，
我们不再是仇敌。
若你愿与我立刻离开家乡，
我愿带一千英镑
让自己身着男装
为自由而战。"

我们是韦克斯福德的小伙儿，
满腔热情地作战
把那恼人的枷锁扯为两半
而解放我们的故土。

我美丽的少女，我不要财富，
而要与你立刻离开家乡。
你那明亮的双眼会是对我的奖励，
对于我来说，比金子更宝贵。
我不要以财富驱动我的手臂
要承担一个好汉之责——
为了解放我的国家，我乐于献出
我心脏里那一滴滴红色血液……副歌

而当我们离开自己的一间间小木屋，小伙儿们，
我们带着十足的善意

To see our friends and neighbours
That were at Vinegar Hill!
A young man from our Irish ranks
A cannon he let go;
He slapped it into Lord Mountjoy
A tyrant he laid low! ... chorus

We bravely fought and conquered
At Ross and Wexford town;
And if we failed to keep them,
'Twas drink that brought us down.
We had no drink beside us
On Tubberneering's day,
Depending on the long, bright pike,
And well it worked that way ... chorus

And Oulart's name shall be their shame,
Whose steel we ne'er did fear.
For every man could do his part
Like Forth and Shelmalier!
And if for want of leaders,
We lost at Vinegar Hill,
We're ready for another fight,
And love our country still!

We are the boys of Wexford,
Who fought with heart and hand
To burst in twain the galling chain
And free our native land.

去探望自己的那些住在
醋山旁的朋友和邻居们！
从我们爱尔兰普通士兵中走出的一个青年
他发射了一门大炮；
他炮击了芒乔伊勋爵府
他干倒了一位暴君！……副歌

我们在罗斯和韦克斯福德镇
勇敢作战和攻克；
尽管我们没能守住它们，
那是酒把我们醉倒了。
在图柏涅林日
我们没有随身带酒，
依靠那明晃晃的长矛，
在那种状态下，长矛很好使……副歌

欧拉将成为他们耻辱的名称，
我们从未畏惧其兵器。
因为每个人都应
像福思和谢尔马利耶那样尽责！
若是因为指挥官们不够多，
我们在醋山失利，
我们愿再打一仗，
依然热爱我们的国家！

我们是韦克斯福德的小伙儿，
满腔热情地作战
把那恼人的枷锁扯为两半
而解放我们的故土。

The Memory of the Dead①

Who fears to speak of Ninety-Eight?
Who blushes at the name?
When cowards mock the patriot's fate,
Who hangs his head for shame?
He's all a knave or half a slave
Who slights his country thus;
But a true man, like you, man,
Will fill your glass with us.

We drink the memory of the brave,
The faithful and the few:
Some lie far off beyond the wave,
Some sleep in Ireland, too;
All, all are gone — but still lives on
The fame of those who died:
All true men, like you, men,
Remember them with pride.

Some on the shores of distant lands
Their weary hearts have laid,
And by the stranger's heedless hands
Their lonely graves were made;
But, though their clay be far away
Beyond the Atlantic foam,
In true men, like you, men,

---

① 作为典故,此歌谣出现于《尤利西斯》和《为芬尼根守灵》,其作者为约翰·凯尔斯·英格拉姆 (John Kells Ingram, 1823—1907)。

纪念死者

谁怕谈论九八起义？
有谁耻于该名称？
当懦夫们嘲笑爱国者的遭遇时，
有谁垂头羞愧？
如此轻视其祖国之人
他全然是一个无赖或半个奴隶；
但是，像你这样，一个真正男人，嘿，
会满上自己的酒杯，与我们一同畅饮。

我们干杯以纪念勇士们，
那些忠诚的支持者和少数人：
有些人葬身于深流的波涛之下，
另有一些人长眠于爱尔兰岛；
他们所有人，所有人都去世了——但是
那些死者的声誉仍继续留存：
所有像你们这样，真正的男人，嘿，
会骄傲地记住他们。

在若干遥远国家的那些海岸上，有些人
已让他们疲惫的心安息，
粗心的异乡人用一只只手
为他们建了一座座孤坟；
但是，虽然他们的躯体在遥远的地方
在大西洋彼岸，
在像你们这样的，真正男人的心中，嘿，

Their spirit's still at home.

The dust of some is Irish earth;
Among their own they rest;
And the same land that gave them birth
Has caught them to her breast;
And we will pray that from their clay
Full many a race may start
Of true men, like you, men,
To act as brave a part.

They rose in dark and evil days
To right their native land;
They kindled here a living blaze
That nothing shall withstand.
Alas, that Might can vanquish Right!
They fell, and pass'd away;
But true men, like you, men,
Are plenty here to-day.

Then here's their memory — may it be
For us a guiding light,
To cheer our strife for liberty,
And teach us to unite!
Through good and ill, be Ireland's still,
Though sad as theirs your fate;
And true men be you, men,
Like those of Ninety-Eight.

他们的灵魂仍在故乡。

他们有些人的尸骨注定会化为爱尔兰泥土；
他们在自己的家乡安息；
而就是他们出生的那片土地
已把他们拥入自己的怀抱；
而我们要祈祷
很多民族会始于
像你们这样的，真正男人的身躯，嘿，
作为勇士而践行。

在黑暗和邪恶时代，他们奋起
以便收复自己的故土：
在这里，他们所点燃的不息烈火
无以抵抗。
唉，强权可胜公理！
他们倒下，并亡故；
但是，像你们这样的，真正的男人，嘿，
当今这里有多着呢。

总之，这是对他们的纪念——或许它
对于我们是一盏指路灯，
为我们争取自由而欢呼，
并教我们团结起来！
不管好赖，你们都属于爱尔兰，
尽管你们会与他们有同样不幸的命运；
你们是真正的男人，嘿，
就像那些九八起义中的义士。

The Minstrel Boy[①]

The original lyrics are as follows:

I

The Minstrel-Boy to the war is gone,

    In the ranks of death you'll find him;

His father's sword he has girded on,

    And his wild harp slung behind him.

"Land of song!" said the warrior-bard,

"Tho' all the world betrays thee,

One sword, at least, thy rights shall guard,

    One faithful harp shall praise thee!"

II

The Minstrel fell! —but the foeman's chain

    Could not bring that proud soul under;

The harp he lov'd ne'er spoke again,

    For he tore its chords asunder;

And said, "No chains shall sully thee,

    Thou soul of love and bravery!

Thy songs were made for the pure and free,

They shall never sound in slavery."

A concentrated, single verse version exists:

---

① 作为典故,此歌谣出现于《尤利西斯》和《为芬尼根守灵》,其作者为托马斯·莫尔(Thomas Moore,1779—1852)。

参见 Wikipedia: https://en.m.wikipedia.org/wiki/The_Minstrel_Boy.

吟游小伙子

原词如下：

一

这位参战的吟游小伙子离世了，
　　你会在亡者名单中找到他；
他腰佩他父亲的剑，
　　背跨可抒发炽烈情感的竖琴。
"歌的国度！"这位战士和吟游诗人说道，
　　"即使全世界背叛你，
至少，有一把剑会维护你的种种权利，
　　有一架可信赖的竖琴会赞美你！"

二

这位吟游者阵亡了！——但敌人的束缚
　　无法打垮那骄傲的心灵；
他所爱的竖琴再也没发出响声，
　　因为他扯断了它的一根根弦；
并说道："重重枷锁都无法玷污你，
　　还有你那充满爱和勇气的灵魂！
你的一首首歌都为纯洁而自由者创作，
　　它们永远不会在屈从中响起。"

一个单节的浓缩本如下：

The minstrel boy to the war is gone,

In the ranks of death ye may find him

His father's sword he hath girded on,

With his wild harp slung along behind him;

Land of Song, the lays of the warrior bard,

May some day sound for thee,

But his harp belongs to the brave and free

And shall never sound in slavery!

During the American Civil War a third verse was written by an unknown author, and is sometimes included in renditions of the song:

The Minstrel Boy will return we pray

When we hear the news we all will cheer it,

The minstrel boy will return one day,

Torn perhaps in body, not in spirit.

Then may he play on his harp in peace,

In a world such as heaven intended,

For all the bitterness of man must cease,

And ev'ry battle must be ended.

(As an allusion, this song appears in *Ulysses* and *Finnegans Wake*.)

这位参战的吟游小伙子离世了，
你会在亡者名单中找到他
他腰佩他父亲的剑，
背跨可抒发炽烈情感的竖琴；
歌的国度，战士和吟游诗人的一首首叙事诗，
但愿在某一天为你响起，
而他的竖琴则属于勇敢和自由者
且永远不会在屈从中响起！

在美国内战期间，第三节出自一位匿名作者，有时也被纳入这首歌的演绎
之中：

我们企盼的这位吟游小伙子将回来
当我们听到这则消息，都会欢呼，
这位吟游小伙子会在某天回来，
或许身体受伤，但神采飞扬。
然后，他可能平静地弹奏自己的竖琴，
在一个有意建成的极乐世界，
人类的全部苦难肯定停止，
一切战争也肯定结束。

She is Far from the Land[①]

She is far from the land
Where her young hero sleeps,
And lovers are round her, sighing;
But coldly she turns
From their gaze, and weeps,
For her heart in his grave is lying.

She sings the wild songs
Of her dear native plains,
Ev'ry note which she loved awakening —
Ah! little they think
Who delight in her strains,
How the heart of the Minstrel
is breaking.

He had lived for his love,
For his country he died,
They were all that to life
Had entwined him —
Nor soon shall the tears
Of his country be dried,
Nor long will his love
Stay behind him.

Oh! make her a grave

---

① 作为典故,此歌谣出现于《尤利西斯》和《为芬尼根守灵》,其作者为托马斯·莫尔(Thomas Moore, 1779—1852)。

| 乔伊斯作品中的
凯尔特歌谣

她远离了这片土地

她远离了这片土地
这里长眠着她的年青英雄，
在她周围，爱慕者们纷纷叹气；
她却冷漠地转身
避开他们的目光而哭泣，
只因她的爱心存在于他的墓穴。

她常唱那些粗野的歌
歌颂她那亲爱的故乡平原，
唱她想唤醒的每个音符——
啊！他们想不出
谁会喜欢她的旋律，
这位吟游歌手的心
那么忧伤。

他为爱而生，
为国而亡，
它们都与他的生命
休戚相关——
他祖国的泪水
不会转瞬就干，
他的爱人
永不背弃他。

哦！在一束束阳光停留的地方

Where the sunbeams rest,

When they promise a glorious morrow;

They'll shine o'er her sleep

Like a smile from the West,

From her own loved

Island of sorrow.

在它们预示着宜人次日之时，

为她建一座墓穴吧；

它们会伴着她的长眠而照耀

恰似来自西方的一抹微笑，

来自她所爱的

悲伤之岛的微笑。

Johnny, I Hardly Knew Ye[①]

When goin' the road to sweet athy, hurroo, hurroo

When goin' the road to sweet athy, hurroo, hurroo

When goin' the road to sweet athy

A stick in me hand and a drop in me eye

A doleful damsel I heard cry

Johnny I hardly knew ye

With your drums and guns and guns and drums, hurroo, hurroo

With your drums and guns and guns and drums, hurroo, hurroo

With your drums and guns and guns and drums

The enemy nearly slew ye

Oh darling dear, ye look so queer

Johnny I hardly knew ye

Where are the eyes that looked so mild, hurroo, hurroo

Where are the eyes that looked so mild, hurroo, hurroo

Where are the eyes that looked so mild

When my poor heart you first beguiled

Why did ye run from me and the child

Oh Johnny, I hardly knew ye

With your drums and guns and guns and drums, hurroo, hurroo

With your drums and guns and guns and drums, hurroo, hurroo

With your drums and guns and guns and drums

The enemy nearly slew ye

---

① 作为典故,此歌谣出现于《为芬尼根守灵》,其作者为约瑟夫·布赖恩·盖根(Joseph Bryan Geoghegan, 1816—1889)。

约翰尼，我差点没认出你

当走在去那可爱的阿赛的路上，呜呜，呜呜
当走在去那可爱的阿赛的路上，呜呜，呜呜
当走在去那可爱的阿赛的路上
手持杖，眼含泪
我听到一个伤心姑娘的哭声
约翰尼，我差点没认出你

你挎着鼓和枪、枪和鼓，呜呜，呜呜
你挎着鼓和枪、枪和鼓，呜呜，呜呜
你挎着鼓和枪、枪和鼓
敌兵差点弄死你
哦，亲爱的宝贝，你看起来好奇怪
约翰尼，我差点没认出你

曾经那么温柔的双眼哪去了，呜呜，呜呜
曾经那么温柔的双眼哪去了，呜呜，呜呜
曾将那么温柔的双眼哪去了
那时，你初次拨动了我可怜的心儿
为什么，你抛下我和那孩子
哦，约翰尼，我差点没认出你

你挎着鼓和枪、枪和鼓，呜呜，呜呜
你挎着鼓和枪、枪和鼓，呜呜，呜呜
你挎着鼓和枪、枪和鼓
敌兵差点弄死你

Oh darling dear, ye look so queer

Johnny I hardly knew ye

Where are the legs we looked you run, hurroo, hurroo

Where are the legs we looked you run, hurroo, hurroo

Where are the legs that looked you run

But first you went to carry a gun

Indeed your dancing days are done

Oh Johnny, I hardly knew ye

With your drums and guns and guns and drums, hurroo, hurroo

With your drums and guns and guns and drums, hurroo, hurroo

With your drums and guns and guns and drums

The enemy nearly slew ye

Oh darling dear, ye look so queer

Johnny I hardly knew ye

Ye haven't an arm, ye haven't a leg, hurroo, hurroo

Ye haven't an arm, ye haven't a leg, hurroo, hurroo

Ye haven't an arm, ye haven't a leg

Ye're an armless, boneless, chickenless egg

You'll have to be left with a bowl out to beg

Oh Johnny I hardly knew ye

I'm happy for to see ye home, hurroo, hurroo

I'm happy for to see ye home, hurroo, hurroo

I'm happy for to see ye home

All from the island of sulloon

So low in flesh, so high in bone

Oh Johnny I hardly knew ye

哦,亲爱的宝贝,你看起来好奇怪
约翰尼,我差点没认出你

我们曾见你奔跑,那双腿哪去了,呜呜,呜呜
我们曾见你奔跑,那双腿哪去了,呜呜,呜呜
我们曾见你奔跑,那双腿哪去了
你却宁愿去扛枪
你那跳舞的日子真是一去不复返了
哦,约翰尼,我差点没认出你

你挎着鼓和枪、枪和鼓,呜呜,呜呜
你挎着鼓和枪、枪和鼓,呜呜,呜呜
你挎着鼓和枪、枪和鼓
敌兵差点弄死你
哦,亲爱的宝贝,你看起来好奇怪
约翰尼,我差点没认出你

你丢了一条胳膊,你丢了一条腿,呜呜,呜呜
你丢了一条胳膊,你丢了一条腿,呜呜,呜呜
你丢了一条胳膊,你丢了一条腿
你是一个无臂、无骨、无畏的家伙
你以后只好孤零零地,拿着碗外出乞讨
哦,约翰尼,我差点没认出你

见你回家,我真为你高兴,呜呜,呜呜
见你回家,我真为你高兴,呜呜,呜呜
见你回家,我真为你高兴
从锡兰岛归来的都
骨瘦嶙峋
哦,约翰尼,我差点没认出你

With your drums and guns and guns and drums, hurroo, hurroo

With your drums and guns and guns and drums, hurroo, hurroo

With your drums and guns and guns and drums

The enemy never slew ye

Oh darling dear, ye look so queer

Johnny I hardly knew ye

你挎着鼓和枪、枪和鼓,呜呜,呜呜

你挎着鼓和枪、枪和鼓,呜呜,呜呜

你挎着鼓和枪、枪和鼓

敌兵差点弄死你

哦,亲爱的宝贝,你看起来好奇怪

约翰尼,我差点没认出你

《为芬尼根守灵》（1939）中的歌谣

Finnegan's Wake[①]

Tim Finnegan lived in Walker Street

An Irish gintleman, mighty odd.

He'd a bit of a brogue, so neat and sweet,

And to rise in the world, Tim carried a hod.

But Tim had a sort of tippling way:

With a love of liquor Tim was born,

And to help him through his work each day,

Took a drop of the creature every morn.

Chorus:

Whack! Hurroo! Now dance to your partner!

Welt the flure, your trotters shake;

Isn't it the truth I've told ye,

Lots of fun at Finnegan's wake?

One morning Tim was rather full,

His head felt heavy and it made him shake

He fell from the ladder and broke his skull,

So they carried him home, his corpse to wake.

They tied him up in a nice clean sheet,

And laid him out upon the bed,

Wid a gallon of whiskey at his feet,

And a barrel of porter at his head.

---

① 作为典故,此诗出现于《为芬尼根守灵》,是一首爱尔兰民谣,见于艾德琳. 格拉欣(Aaline lasheen)所著《〈为芬尼根守灵〉普查:人物及其角色索引》(*A Census of Finnegans Wake: An Index of the Characters and Their Roles*, London: Faber & Fa ber Limited, 1956)第 40 页。

为芬尼根守灵①

以前，蒂姆·芬尼根居住在沃尔克街
他是一位十分古怪的爱尔兰绅士。
他的英文略带爱尔兰土腔，听起来温柔而甜蜜，
蒂姆是运砖工，渴望有一天能飞黄腾达。
但是，蒂姆有一种饮酒习惯：
蒂姆生来爱酒，
每天清晨一口酒，
助他度过一天工作时光。

副歌：
敲击！欢呼！与伴一同随歌起舞！
音乐奏起来，脚步动起来；
为芬尼根守灵时，有过好多笑话，
对你，我讲过那件真事儿，不是吗？

一天早上，蒂姆喝多了，
他头昏脑胀，摇摇晃晃
他从梯子上坠落，摔破了头，
因此，他们将他抬回家，为他守灵。
他们用一张干净漂亮的床单将他捆绑好，
让他躺在床上，
一加仑的威士忌放在他的脚边，
搬运工的桶也摆在他床头。

---

① 该诗歌译文的第三节和末节参见、引用冯建明：《乔伊斯长篇小说人物塑造》（北京：人民文学出版社，2010 年）第 179 页。

His friends assembled at his wake.

Missus Finnegan called out for lunch:

And first they laid in tay and cake,

Then pipes and tobaccy and whiskey punch.

Miss Biddy Moriarty began to cay;

"Such a purty corpse did yez ever see?

Arrah, Tim mavourneen, an' why did ye die?"

"Hold yer gob," sez Judy Magee.

Then Peggy O'Connor took up the job,

"Arrah, Biddy," sez she, "yer wrong, I'm sure."

But Biddy gave her a belt in the flure.

Each side in war did soon engage;

'Twas woman to woman and man to man;

Shillelah law was all the rage,

And a bloody ruction soon began.

Micky Maloney raised his head,

When a gallon a whisky flew at him;

It missed, and falling on the bed,

The liguor scattered over Tim.

"Och, he revives! See how he raises!"

And Timothy, jumping up from bed,

Sez, "Whirl your liquor around like blazes —

Souls to the devil! D'ye think I'm dead?"

他的朋友聚在一起，为他守灵。
蒂姆的老婆召集大家吃午餐：
先奉上茶水与蛋糕，
随后是馅饼、香烟和威士忌潘趣酒。
比迪·莫里亚蒂小姐开始大哭；
"你们谁见过这么干净的尸体？
啊呀，蒂姆宝贝，你怎么就这么离开了？"
"闭嘴吧，"朱迪·马吉说。

接着，轮到佩吉·奥康纳了，
"啊呀，"她说："你错了，我肯定。"
但是，比迪抽了她一耳光。
一场战役一触即发；
这是女人与女人，男人与男人之间的较量；
斗殴泄怒，
一场血腥的骚动即将上演。

米基·马洛尼抬起头，
这时，一加仑容量的威士忌酒瓶砸向他；
酒瓶没砸中人，跌落床上，
酒水洒在蒂姆身上。
"天哪，他复活了！看，他竟起身了！"
蒂莫西从床上一跃而起，
说道："你们竟然到处洒酒——
活见鬼！你们以为我死了？"

In the Name of Annah the Allmaziful[①]

(Song Lyrics in *Finnegans Wake by James Joyce*)

In the name of Annah the Allmaziful,

the Everliving, the Bringer of Plurabilities,

haloed be her eve,

her singtime sung,

her rill be run,

unhemmed as it is uneven!

Her untitled mamafesta

memorialising

the Mosthighest has gone by many names at disjointed times.

---

① 此歌词由乔伊斯创作,是《为芬尼根守灵》第 104 页中的文字,其原文为散文形式,无标题。

奉安娜之名，她自古就存在①

(詹姆斯·乔伊斯小说《为芬尼根守灵》中的诗句)

奉安娜之名，她自古就存在，
永生，多能，
光轮照耀她出现的傍晚，
赞美她的圣歌飘扬，
小溪流淌，
她无论如何永不受妨碍！

她的无名宣言
是铭记
那全盘错乱时代拥有诸多名字的至尊者。

---

① 该诗歌译文参见、引用冯建明：《乔伊斯长篇小说人物塑造》(北京：人民文学出版社，2010
年)第195页。

Nuvoletta in Her Light Dress[①]

(Song Lyrics in *Finnegans Wake by James Joyce*)

Nuvoletta in her light dress,

spunn of sisteen shimmers,

was looking down on them,

leaning over the bannistars

and list'ning all she childishly could.

. . .

She was alone.

All her nubied companions

were asleeping with the squir'ls.

. . .

She tried all the winsome wonsome ways

her four winds had taught her.

She tossed her sfumastelliacinous hair

like *la princesse de la Petite Bretagne*

and she rounded her mignons arms

like Missis Cornwallis-West

and she smiled over herself

like the image of the pose

of the daughter of the queen of the Emperour of Irelande

and she sighed after herself as were she born

to bride with Tristis Tristior ristissimus.

But, sweet madonnine, she might fair as well

have carried her daisy's worth to Florida.

. . .

---

① 此歌词由乔伊斯创作,是《为芬尼根守灵》第 157—159 页中的文字,其原文为散文形式,无标题。

披睡衣的努沃莱塔

（詹姆斯·乔伊斯小说《为芬尼根守灵》中的诗句）

披睡衣的努沃莱塔，

悠然自在十六夏，

曾俯视栏杆，

斜倚扶手，

未脱稚气，倾听万籁。

……

她曾形单影只。

她可爱的伙伴们

都正与那群松鼠同眠。

……

她曾试着用四风所授的

各种花式的绰约风姿。

她像布列塔尼公主那样

甩了甩蓬松秀发

如帕特里克·坎贝尔夫人一般

环抱娇美的双臂

她嫣然一笑

模样宛如

爱尔兰的那位公主

她忾然叹息，百结愁肠，

仿佛生当作特里斯坦新娘。

然而，可爱、端庄、美丽的淑女会

以贞洁之躯赴佛罗里达。

……

Oh, how it was duusk. From Vallee Maraia to Grasyaplaina,
dormimust echo! Ah dew! Ah dew!
It was so duusk that the tears of night began to fall,
first by ones and twos, then by threes and fours,
at last by fives and sixes of sevens,
for the tired ones were wecking,
as we weep now with them. O! O! *Par la pluie*.

. . .

Then Nuvoletta reflected for the last time
in her little long life
and she made up all her myriads of drifting minds in one.
She cancelled all her engauzements.
She climbed over the bannistars;
she gave a childy cloudy cry: *Nuée*! *Nuée*!
A light dress fluttered.
She was gone.

嘿,天色多么暗淡。从马拉雅山谷到格拉西亚草原,

寂静中的回声! 啊,再会! 啊,再会!

天色如此暗淡,夜雨始落,

先是每次一两滴,接着每次三四滴,

最终每次五六七滴,

由于那些疲倦者被吵醒,

如同我们正与其同哀。哦! 哦! 被雨声吵醒!

……

然后,努沃莱塔在短暂的人生阶段中

最后一次思索

就把她那漂浮的万千思绪聚成一体。

她取消所有约会。

她翻越扶手;

她如孩子般,发出一声模糊的叫喊:雨云! 雨云!

睡衣飘动。

她不见了。

Slipping Sly by Sallynoggin[①]

(Song Lyrics in *Finnegans Wake by James Joyce*)

... slipping sly by Sallynoggin,

as happy as the day is wet,

babbling, bubbling, chattering to herself,

deloothering the fields on their elbows

leaning with the sloothering slide of her,

giddygaddy, grannyma, gossipaceous Anna Livia.

He lifts the lifewand and the dumb speak.

— Quoiquoiquoiquoiquoiquoiquoiq!

---

① 此歌词由乔伊斯创作,是《为芬尼根守灵》第 195 页中的文字,其原文为散文形式,无标题。

偷偷地经莎莉诺金而下①

（詹姆斯·乔伊斯小说《为芬尼根守灵》中的诗句）

……偷偷地经莎莉诺金而下，

美不滋儿地像遇到雨天似的，

嘀嘀咕咕，唧唧哝哝，唠唠叨叨地自言自语，

哗哗地拐过田野的急转弯处

河面随汩汩的水流的转动而倾斜，

这卖弄风情、优游逍遥的老奶奶、喋喋不休的安娜·利维娅。

他举起生命魔杖，哑巴也讲话。

——啥啥啥啥啥啥啥！

---

① 该诗歌译文参见、引用冯建明：《乔伊斯长篇小说人物塑造》（北京：人民文学出版社，2010
年）第 176 页。

O[1]

（Song Lyrics in *Finnegans Wake by James Joyce*）

O

tell me all about

Anna Livia! I want to hear all

about Anna Livia. Well，you know Anna Livia? Yes，of course，we all

know Anna Livia. Tell me all. Tell me now.

---

① 此歌词由乔伊斯创作，是《为芬尼根守灵》第 196 页中的文字，无标题，排列成一个三角形。该三角象征一个三角洲。在此三角洲，两个洗衣妇一边洗衣，一边议论安娜。可见，三角洲是安娜的艺术形象之一。在现代诗歌中，句子常被排成几何形，来表现某种寓意。故而，此处的"三角形"可视为现代诗行。

噢①

（詹姆斯·乔伊斯小说《为芬尼根守灵》中的诗句）

噢

给我说说所有关于

安娜·利维娅的事儿！我想听听所有

关于安娜·利维娅的事儿。喔，你了解安娜·利维娅吗？嗯，当然，我们都
了解安娜·利维娅。给我说说每件事儿。现在就说给我听。

---

① 该诗歌译文参见、引用冯建明：《乔伊斯长篇小说人物塑造》（北京：人民文学出版社，2010
年）第 121 页。

Wharnow are Alle Her Childer, Say?[①]

（Song Lyrics in *Finnegans Wake by James Joyce*）

Wharnow are alle her childer, say?

In kingdome gone

or power to come

or gloria be to them farther?

Allalivial, allalluvial!

Some here,

more no more,

more again lost alla stranger.

---

① 此歌词由乔伊斯创作,是《为芬尼根守灵》第 213 页中的文字,其原文为散文形式,无标题。

现在，她的孩子们去哪儿了，啊？[1]

（詹姆斯·乔伊斯小说《为芬尼根守灵》中的诗句）

现在，她的孩子们去哪儿了，啊？

是去追寻那早已消失的王国了

或是去追逐未来的权势了

还是去将荣耀献给浪迹天涯的人了？

哈利路亚，哈利路亚！

在他们当中，有的仍在世，

更多的已谢世，

还有更多的在异乡迷了路。

---

[1] 该诗歌译文参见、引用冯建明：《乔伊斯长篇小说人物塑造》（北京：人民文学出版社，2010年）第 243 页。

Tys Elvenland!^①

(Song Lyrics in *Finnegans Wake by James Joyce*)

Tys Elvenland!

Teems of times and happy returns.

The seim anew.

Ordovico or viricordo.

Anna was，Livia is，Plurabelle's to be.

仙境！①

（詹姆斯·乔伊斯小说《为芬尼根守灵》中的歌词）

仙境！

时间长河，长命百岁。

你也一样。

我记得你。

过去是安娜，现在是利维娅，将来是普卢拉贝勒（ALP）。

---

① 该诗歌译文参见、引用冯建明：《乔伊斯长篇小说人物塑造》（北京：人民文学出版社，2010年）第 215 页。

Lowly, Longly, a Wail Went Forth[①]

(Song Lyrics in *Finnegans Wake by James Joyce*)

Lowly, longly, a wail went forth.

Pure Yawn lay low.

On the mead of the hillock lay,

heartsoul dormant mid shadowed landshape⋯

---

① 此歌词由乔伊斯创作,是《为芬尼根守灵》第 474 页中的文字,其原文为散文形式,无标题。

低声地，长久地，一声哀号响起①

(詹姆斯·乔伊斯小说《为芬尼根守灵》中的诗句)

低声地，长久地，一声哀号响起。

纯洁的亚恩去世了。

他躺在小丘草地上，

安眠于洒满荫影的景色中……

---

① 该诗歌译文参见、引用冯建明：《乔伊斯长篇小说人物塑造》(北京：人民文学出版社，2010
年)第 243 页。

Dream[①]

(Song Lyrics in *Finnegans Wake by James Joyce*)

Dream.

Ona nonday I sleep.

I dreamt of a somday.

Of a wonday I shall wake.

———————————

① 此歌词由乔伊斯创作,是《为芬尼根守灵》第 481 页中的文字,其原文为散文形式,无标题。

梦

（詹姆斯·乔伊斯小说《为芬尼根守灵》中的诗句）

梦。
俄南啊，一天，我会睡着。
某一天，我会进入梦乡。
总有一天，我会醒来。

I'm Getting Mixed[①]

(Song Lyrics in *Finnegans Wake by James Joyce*)

I'm getting mixed.

Brightening up and tightening down.

Yes, you're changing,

sonhusband, and you're turning,

I can feel you,

for a daughterwife from the hills again.

Imlamaya.

And she is coming.

---

① 此歌词由乔伊斯创作,是《为芬尼根守灵》第 626 至 627 页中的文字,其原文为散文形式,无标题。

我在被融合①

（詹姆斯·乔伊斯小说《为芬尼根守灵》中的诗句）

我在被融合。
河面发亮,河水奔腾而下。
嗯,你在变,
像儿子一样的丈夫,你在转,
我能感觉到你的想法,
从群山中,再找一个像女儿一样的妻子。
从整条喜马拉雅山脉。
她要来了。

---

① 该诗歌译文参见、引用冯建明：《乔伊斯长篇小说人物塑造》（北京：人民文学出版社,2010
年）第240页。

... My Cold Father[①]

(Song Lyrics in *Finnegans Wake by James Joyce*)

... my cold father,

my cold mad father,

my cold mad feary father,

till the near sight of the mere size of him,

the moyles and moyles of it,

moananoaning, makes me seasilt saltsick

and I rush, my only, into your arms.

...

Far calls.

Coming, far!

---

① 此歌词由乔伊斯创作,是《为芬尼根守灵》第 628 页中的文字,其原文为散文形式,无标题。

……我冷酷的父亲

（詹姆斯·乔伊斯小说《为芬尼根守灵》中的诗句）

……我冷酷的父亲，

我冷酷而鲁莽的父亲，

我冷酷、鲁莽而可怕的父亲，

直到近距离看到他的真面目，

数英里的海水，

咆哮着，使我晕眩

于是，我的唯一，我急忙，投入您的怀中。

……

父亲在呼唤。

来了，父亲！

End Here[①]

(Song Lyrics in *Finnegans Wake by James Joyce*)

End here.

Us then. Finn，again!

Take. Bussoftlhee，

mememormee! Till thousendsthee.

Lps. The keys to. Given!

A way

a lone a last a loved a long the

---

① 此歌词由乔伊斯创作，是《为芬尼根守灵》结尾的文字，其原文为散文形式，无标题。

到此为止①

（詹姆斯·乔伊斯小说《为芬尼根守灵》中的诗句）

到此为止。
我们于是。《为芬尼根守灵》！
拿着。但要轻轻地，
记着我！直到千年。
我将给你天堂的那些钥匙！
一条路
一条孤独的一条最终的一条人人爱的一条漫长的

---

① 该诗歌译文参见、引用冯建明：《乔伊斯长篇小说人物塑造》（北京：人民文学出版社，2010年）第 246 页。

The Dawn Awakes with Tremulous Alarms[①]

^cThe dawn awakes with tremulous alarms,
  How grey, how could, how bare!
O, hold me still white arms, encircling arms!
  And hide me, heave hair!

Life is a dream, a dream. The hour is done
  And antiphon is said.
We go from the light and falsehood of the sun
  To bleak wastes of the dead.^c

---

① 此诗出现在乔伊斯所著 *Stephen Hero*. Ed. Theodore Spencer. Rev. ed. (London: The Alden Press, 1956)第42页,其原文没有题目。此诗译文参见和引用冯建明等译的《斯蒂芬英雄:〈艺术家年轻时的写照〉初稿的一部分》(上海:三联书店,2019 年),其题目由编译者添加。

伴着阵阵颤抖的铃声，黎明醒来

^{（约）}伴着阵阵颤抖的铃声，黎明醒来，
何等灰暗，何等阴冷，何等空旷！
哦，用白色的双臂、环抱着的双臂搂住我吧！
也用浓发遮挡我吧！

人生是一场梦，一场梦。那一小时的宗教仪式结束了
一小段赞美诗也被朗诵。
我们从圣灵亮光和日光假象中走出
迈向死者那清冷的荒原。^{（约）}

My Ideal[①]

Art thou real, my Ideal?
Wilt thou ever come to me
In the soft and gentle twilight
With your baby on your knee?

---

① 此诗出现在乔伊斯所著 *Stephen Hero*. Ed. Theodore Spencer. Rev. ed. （London：The Alden Press，1956)第 87 页。此诗译文参见和引用冯建明等译的《斯蒂芬英雄:〈艺术家年轻时的写照〉初稿的一部分》(上海：三联书店,2019 年)。

我心中完美的人

　　我心中完美的人，你真有此意？
你是否愿来找我
在那温柔与平和的黄昏
让你的宝贝儿坐在你膝上？

Shall Carry My Heart to Thee[①]

Shall carry my heart to thee,

Shall carry my heart to thee,

And the breath of the balmy night

Shall carry my heart to thee.

---

① 此诗出现在乔伊斯所著 *Stephen Hero*. Ed. Theodore Spencer. Rev. ed. （London：The Alden Press，1956)第 165 页和 Stanislaus Joyce 所著 *My Brother's Keeper*：*James Joyce's Early Years*（New York：The Viking Press，1969）第 122 页。本书所引用的原文依据 *Stephen Hero* 中的版本。此诗译文参见和引用冯建明等译的《看守我兄长的人：詹姆斯·乔伊斯的早期生活》(上海：上海三联书店,2019 年)和《斯蒂芬英雄：〈艺术家年轻时的写照〉初稿的一部分》(上海：三联书店,2019 年)。

欲将吾爱心交付汝

欲将吾爱心交付汝，
欲将吾爱心交付汝，
以及那温暖宜人夜晚之微风
欲将吾爱心交付汝。

《乔伊斯书信集》中的歌谣

Song①

（for music）

Ah，the sighs that come from my heart

They grieve me passing sore!

Sith I must from my love depart

Farewell，my joy，for evermore.

I was wont her to behold

And clasp in armes twain.

And now with sighes manifold

Farewell my joy and welcome pain!

Ah methinks that could I yet

（As would to God I might!）

There would no joy compare with it

Unto my heart to make it light.

---

① 此诗后 4 行出现在詹姆斯·乔伊斯于 1904 年 7 月写给诺拉·巴那克尔的信中。此信见理查
德·艾尔曼编辑的《乔伊斯书信选》。

歌

（为谱乐）

啊,那一声声叹息发自我心中
它们叫我沉溺于昔日伤痛!
从此,我必须离开我所爱的人
别了,我的快乐,直到永远。

以前,我常常注视着她
还用双臂,把她紧紧拥抱。
而今,仅余不已嗟叹
别了,我的快乐! 去迎接痛苦吧!

啊,我认为自己无法再拥有
(或许,我到上帝那里,才会拥有!)
无法再拥有类似的欢乐
致使我内心让它淡漠。

I Saw My Lady Weep[①]

I saw my lady weep,

And Sorrow proud to be advanced so,

In those fair eyes where all perfections keep.

Her face was full of woe,

But such a woe (believe me) as wins more hearts,

Than Mirth can do with her enticing parts.

Sorrow was there made fair,

And Passion wise, tears a delightful thing,

Silence beyond all speech a wisdom rare.

She made her sighs to sing,

And all things with so sweet a sadness move,

As made my heart at once both grieve and love.

O fairer than aught else

The world can show, leave off in time to grieve.

Enough, enough, your joyful looks excels.

Tears kill the heart, believe;

O strive not to be excellent in woe,

Which only breeds your beauty's overthrow.

---

① 此诗的末 3 行出现在詹姆斯·乔伊斯 1909 年 11 月 1 日给诺拉·巴那克尔的信中,其作者为
约翰·道兰(John Dowland, 1563—1626)。此信见理查德·艾尔曼编辑的《乔伊斯书信选》。

我看到我爱人流泪

我看到我爱人流泪，
悲伤让她愈加秀美，
那双凤眸顾盼生辉。
她愁容满面，
这种哀怨（相信我）则更能拨动人心，
胜过她那迷人的欢笑。

悲伤使人美丽，
受难使人明智，泪水使人痛快，
沉默乃非凡智慧，强于一切言语。
她以叹为歌，
万物皆因忧伤而极柔，
恰似我心于感伤之时，亦生爱慕之情。

哦，在这世上
你拥有绝色之美，及时停止伤心吧。
你快乐时的容貌出类拔萃，够了吧，够了吧。
泪水令人心碎，相信吧；
哦，勿力求过度悲伤，
悲伤只会令你美丽不再。

Rouen Is the Rainiest Place Getting[①]

Rouen is the rainiest place getting

Inside all impermeables, wetting

Damp marrow in drenched bones.

Midwinter soused us coming over Le Mans

Our inn at Niort was the Grape of Burgunfy

But the winepress of the Lord thundered over that grape of Burgundy

And we left it in a hurgundy.

      (Hurry up, Joyce, it's time!)

I heard mosquitoes swarm in old Bordeaux

So many!

I had not thought the earth contained so many

      (Hurry up, Joyce, it's time)

Mr Anthologos, the local gardener,

Greycapped, with politeness full of cunning

Has made wine these fifty years

And told me in his southern Frence

Le petit vin is the surest drink to buy

For if'tis bad

Vous ne l'avez pas paye

      (Hurry up, hurry up, now, now, now!)

But we shall have great times,

---

① 这是托马斯·斯特恩斯·艾略特（THOMAS STEARNS Eliot, 1888—1965）《荒原》（*The Waste Land*, 1922）的戏仿作品。此诗见于 1925 年 8 月 15 日詹姆斯·乔伊斯写给哈丽特·肖·韦弗的信中。该诗在此信中没有题目。此信见理查德·艾尔曼编辑的 *Selected Letters of James Joyce*（New York：The Viking Press, 1975）.。

鲁昂是雨水最丰沛的地方

鲁昂是雨水最丰沛的地方
使片片防渗层内都变湿
湿透了骨，弄潮了髓。
我们从勒芒来，却被仲冬淋个透
在尼奥尔，我们住勃艮第葡萄客栈
但上帝榨酒机的轰鸣掠过那勃艮第葡萄
于是，我们就赶紧离开那儿。
　　（快点，乔伊斯，该走了！）

在古老的波尔多，我听到蚊群的嗡嗡声
太多了！
我从没想到世上竟有这么多
　　（快点，乔伊斯，该走了）

安索格勒斯先生，当地园丁，
头顶灰帽，有礼又灵巧
已酿酒长达五十年
用他那南部法语告诉我
小红酒务必得买下
它若是质劣的
就白送给你
　　（快点，快点，立刻，立刻，立刻！）

但是，我们会玩得很开心，

When we return to Clinic, that waste land
O Esculapios!
　　（Shan't we? Shan't we? Shan't we?）

当我们返回诊所,那片荒地

哦,神医!

（我们不回去？我们不回去？我们不回去？）

Goodbye, Zurich, I Must Leave You[①]

Goodbye, Zurich, I must leave you,

Though it breaks my heart to shreds

Tat then attat. [②]

Something tells me I am needed

In Paree to hump the beds.

Bump! I hear the trunks a tumbling

And I'm frantic for the fray.

Farewell, dolce far niente!

Goodbye, Zurichsee![③]

---

① 此诗见于 1934 年 11 月 28 日詹姆斯·乔伊斯写给乔治和海伦·乔伊斯信中。该诗在此信中没有题目。

② Imitation of drum taps.

③ As Stuart Gilbert points out, this is a parody of a patriotic song, 'Dolly Gray', of the same vintage as 'The Absent-minded Beggar' referred to in *Ulysses*. The refrain ran:

Good-bye, Dolly, I must leave you,

Though it breaks my heart to go.

Something tells me I am needed

In the front to face the foe.

Hark! I hear the bugles calling

And I must no longer stay.

Good-bye, Dolly, I must leave you,

Good-bye, Dolly Gray.

再见吧，苏黎世，我必须离开你

再见吧，苏黎世，我必须离开你，

虽然离开会让我心碎

咚不隆咚①。

有些事情暗示：需要我

在巴黎搬运一张张床。

砰！我听到那些大箱子倒下的声音

于是，我很担心那些大箱子受损。

告别了，无所事事的快乐！

再见吧，苏黎世湖！②

---

① 模仿一阵鼓点。

② 正像斯图尔特·吉尔伯特所言：这是对爱国歌曲《多莉·格雷》的戏仿作品。在《尤利西斯》
中，同一歌曲被称为《那个心不在焉的乞丐》。副歌为：
再见吧，多莉，我必须离开你，
虽然离开会让我心碎。
有些事情暗示：需要我
上前线，去对付敌人。
听！我听到阵阵军号在召唤
于是，我决不可再停留。
再见吧，多莉，我必须离开你，
再见吧，多莉·格雷。

《看守我兄长的人》（1958）中乔伊斯的诗歌①

---

① 本书中，选自《看守我兄长的人：詹姆斯·乔伊斯的早期生活》中的诗歌。译文参见和引用冯建明等译的《看守我兄长的人：詹姆斯·乔伊斯的早期生活》（上海：上海三联书店，2019年）和冯建明著的《乔伊斯长篇小说人物塑造》（北京：人民文学出版社，2010年）内容。

Et Tu, Healy[①]

His quaint-perched aerie on the crags of Time
Where the rude din of this ... century
Can trouble him no more.

---

① 此诗见斯坦尼斯劳斯·乔伊斯(Stanislaus Joyce，1884—1955)所著《看守我兄长的人：詹姆斯·乔伊斯的早期生活》(*My Brother's Keeper：James Joyce's Early Years*，New York：The Viking Press，1958)第 46 页。

还有你，希利

他那古雅的鹰巢坐落于时代险崖
在那里，这……世纪粗鲁的喧嚣声
再无法打扰他。

Rebuking[①]

Am I foolish to be hopin'
That you left your window open
To be listenin' to me mopin'
Here and singin', lady mine?

---

① 此诗见斯坦尼斯劳斯·乔伊斯(Stanislaus Joyce，1884—1955)所著《看守我兄长的人：詹姆斯·乔伊斯的早期生活》(*My Brother's Keeper*：*James Joyce's Early Years*，New York：The Viking Press，1958)第 86 页。

责备

我能傻傻地期望
你开着窗
听着我在这儿徘徊
和唱歌吗，我的心上人？

A Goldschmidt Swam in a Kriegsverein[①]

A Goldschmidt swam in a Kriegsverein

As wise little Goldschmidts do,

And he loved every scion of the Habsburg line,

Each Archduke proud, the whole jimbang crowd.

And he felt that they loved him, too.

Herr Rosenbaum and Rosenfeld

And every other Feld except Schlachtfeld;

All worked like niggers, totting rows of crazy figures,

To save Kaiser Karl and Goldschmidt, too.

Chorus:

For he said it is bet-bet-better

To stick stamps on some God-damned letter

Than be shot in a trench

Amid shells and stench,

Jesus Gott-Donner wet-wet-wetter.

---

① 此诗见于理查德・艾尔曼(Richard Ellmann)所著《乔伊斯传》(*James Joyce.* New and Rev. ed. Oxford: Oxford University Press, 1983)第 420 页,其原文没有题目。

一个名叫戈尔德施密的人曾在战争部门忙活

一个名叫戈尔德施密的人曾在战争部门忙活
正如许多名叫戈尔德施密的聪明小人物一样，
他热爱哈布斯堡家族的每一位子弟，
每一个骄傲的王公、家族的整个群体。
他觉得他们也待见他。
包括罗森鲍姆先生以及罗森菲尔德先生
还有一个，叫他什么菲尔德都行，就是别叫他希拉特菲尔德就行；
都像黑人那样干活，积攒着一排又一排疯狂数字，
以便救助卡尔皇帝和戈尔德施密。

合唱：
因为他说赌—赌—更棒
给某一封遭上帝诅咒的信贴几张邮票
也比在到处是炮弹和臭气的
战壕内被射杀来得好，
耶稣啊，天哪，有这样的事儿。

The C. G. Is Not Literary[①]

Up to rheumy Zurich came an Irishman one day,

And as the town was rather dull he thought he'd give a play,

So that the German propagandists might be rightly riled,

But the bully British Philistine once more drove Oscar Wilde.

    CHORUS: Oh, the C. G. is not literary,

            And his handymen are rogues.

            The C. G.'s about as literary

            As an Irish kish of brogues.

            We have paid up all expenses

            As the good Swiss Public knows,

            But we'll be damned well damned before we pay for

            Private Carr's swank hose.

When the play was over Carr with rage began to dance,

Saying I want twenty quid for them there dandy pants,

So fork us out the tin or Comrade Bennett here and me,

We're going to wing your bloody necks, we're out for liberty.

    CHORUS: As before.

They found a Norse solicitor to prove that white was black,

That one can boss in Switzerland beneath the Union Jack;

They went off to the Gerichtshof, but came back like Jack and Jill

For the pants came tumbling after, and the judge is laughing still.

---

① 此诗见于理查德·艾尔曼(Richard Ellmann)所著《乔伊斯传》(*James Joyce*. New and Rev. ed. Oxford: Oxford University Press, 1983)第 445—446 页。

那位总领事与文学无缘

一天，一个爱尔兰男人来到阴冷的苏黎世，
因为这镇子当时很无聊，他就想找个乐子玩，
好让德国的那些宣传家不爽，
不料，那位霸道的不列颠俗货再次排挤奥斯卡·王尔德。

　　　副歌：哦，那位总领事与文学无缘，
　　　　　　而他的手下个个都是无赖。
　　　　　　那位总领事对文学
　　　　　　算得上是浅见寡识。
　　　　　　我们偿付了各项开销
　　　　　　对于这一点，善良的瑞士民众是知道的，
　　　　　　但是，我们若要为列兵卡尔花哨的裤子买单
　　　　　　那可就太缺心眼了。

当那场戏演完，卡尔就开始暴跳如雷，
说"我要 20 英镑去买时装裤，
因此，赶紧给我们掏钱，否则，我找战友班奈特过来，
我们会拧断你们的脖子，我们这完全是为了自由。"

　　　副歌：同上

他们找了个挪威律师来颠倒黑白，
在瑞士，那位英国佬有时会指手画脚；
他们走出门，跑到国际法庭，却狼狈而回
因为他们的裤子松掉，逗得那位法官大笑。

CHORUS: Oh，the C. G. is not literary，

And his handymen are rogues.

The C. G. 's about as literary

As an Irish kish of brogues

So farewell，bruiser Bnnett，

And goodbye，Chummy Carr，

If you put a begger up on horseback，

Why'e dunno where 'e are.

副歌：哦，那位总领事与文学无缘，

　　　而他的手下个个都是无赖。

　　　那位总领事对文学

　　　算得上是浅见寡识

　　　那么，告别了，好勇斗狠的本内特，

　　　再见吧，卡尔老伙计，

　　　一个叫花子一旦被抬举，

　　　竟忘了自己算个老几。

Man dear, did you never hear of buxom Molly Bloom at all

As plump an Irish beauty, sir, as Annie Levy Blumenthal,

If she sat in the vice-regal box Tim Healy'd have no room at all,

    But curl up in a corner at a glance from her eye.

The tale of her ups and downs would aisy fill a handybook

That would cover the whole world across form Gib right on to Sandy Hook,

But now that tale is told, alone, I've lost my daring dandy look

    Since Molly Bloom has gone and left me here to die.

Man dear, I remember when my roving time was troubling me

We picnicked fine in storm or shine in France and Spain and Hungary,

And she said I'd be her first and last while the wine I poured went bubbling

free.

    Now every male she meets with has a finger in her pie.

Man dear, I remember how with all the heart and bane of me.

I arrayed her for the bridal, but, oh, she proved the bane of me,

With more puppies sniffing round her than the wooers of Penelope

    She's left me on the doorstep like a dog for to die.

My left eye is awash and his neighbour full of water, man,

I cannot see the lass I limned for Ireland's gamest daughter, man,

When I hear her lovers tumbling in their thousands for to court her, man,

    If I were sure I'd not be seen I'd sit down and cry.

May you live, may you love like this gaily spinning earth of ours,

---

① 这是一支歌曲《莫莉·布兰尼根》的戏仿作品，为致敬《尤利西斯》中的莫莉·布卢姆。作为典故，此诗见于理查德·艾尔曼（Richard Ellmann）所著《乔伊斯传》（*James Joyce*. New and Rev. ed. Oxford: Oxford University Press, 1983）第 549—550 页。

（致《摩莉·布兰尼根》曲）

好哥们儿，你压根没听说过丰满的摩莉·布卢姆吧

她是爱尔兰美人，先生啊，她就像安妮·利维·布卢门撒尔那样圆润，

以前，若她在总督包厢里坐下，蒂姆·希利可就没处可待啦，

  只能缩在一个角落，受她的冷眼。

她的曲折经历能轻易写满一册

包含的内容从直布罗陀到桑迪胡克，遍布全球，

然而，如今讲完了她的经历，唉，我再也不能耍大酷了

  因为摩莉·布卢姆走了，把我撂在这儿等死。

好哥们儿，我记得自己曾一度漂泊不安

在法国、西班牙和匈牙利，无论晴雨天，我们都快乐地野餐，

她曾说：只要我给她把盏，让她尽欢，我就是她最初和最终的侣伴。

  如今，她所遇见的每个男人都勾搭她。

好哥们儿，我还记得如何用尽心思和脑力。

我曾给她张罗新婚妆扮，但是，唉，她竟然是我的灾星，

讨好她的傲慢小子那么多，其数量比珀涅罗珀的追求者还多

  她把我撇弃在门阶旁，让我像狗一样等死。

我左眼水汪汪，我右眼也泪盈眶，哥们儿啊，

我不能看见我所描写的爱尔兰最果敢的女孩，哥们儿啊，

我听说她那数以千计的情人在向她求婚，哥们儿啊，

  但愿我能找个没人处坐下哭一场。

愿你像我们这个旋转地球那样快乐地生活和恋爱，

And every morn a gallous son awake you to fresh wealth of gold,

But if I cling like a child to the clouds that are your petticoats,

O Molly, handsome Molly, sure you won't let me die?

每天早晨,一个淘气小孩叫醒你,让你收获新财富,
但是,若我像一个孩子一样拉着你那云团般的层层衬裙,
　　哦,摩莉,靓丽的摩莉,你肯定不会让我死去吧?

詹姆斯·乔伊斯年谱

冯建明

1882 年 （出生）	2 月 2 日，詹姆斯·奥古斯丁·阿洛伊修斯·乔伊斯（James Augustine Aloysius Joyce）出生于爱尔兰都柏林市郊拉斯加（Rathgar）布莱顿区西街（Brighton Square West）41 号，其父约翰·斯坦尼斯劳斯·乔伊斯（John Stanislaus Joyce，1849—1931）是税务员。这位税务员与其妻玛丽·简（梅）·默里·乔伊斯（Mary Jane (May) Murray Joyce，1859—1903）共生了 15 个孩子。在这 15 个孩子中，有 10 个活了下来，詹姆斯·乔伊斯在这 10 个孩子中年龄最大。 2 月 5 日，詹姆斯·乔伊斯在一个偏远教区郎德汤（Roundtown）的圣约瑟小教堂（St. Joseph's Chapel of Ease）受洗，施洗牧师是约翰·奥马洛伊（John O'Mulloy）。 5 月，弗雷德里克·卡文迪施勋爵（Lord Frederick Cavendish，1836—1882）和托马斯·亨利·伯克（Thomas Henry Burke，1829—1882）在都柏林的凤凰公园（Phoenix Park）遇刺。
1884 年 （2 岁）	4 月，乔伊斯一家从布莱顿区迁居至都柏林市郊拉斯曼司（Rathmines）的卡斯尔伍德大道（Castlewood Avenue）23 号。在乔伊斯一家的多次迁居中，这次是第一次。 乔伊斯一家自 1884 年 4 月至 1887 年 4 月居住在拉斯曼司。 1884 年 12 月 17 日，詹姆斯·乔伊斯的胞弟约翰·斯坦尼斯劳斯（斯坦尼）·乔伊斯（John Stanislaus "Stannie" Joyce，1884—1955）出生。在詹姆斯·乔伊斯健在的兄弟姐妹 9 人中，他与斯坦尼斯劳斯·乔伊斯的关系最亲密。
1886 年 （4 岁）	英国首相兼自由党领袖威廉·尤尔特·格拉德斯通（William Ewart Gladstone，1809—1898）《自治法案》（Home Rule Bill）未获通过。
1887 年 （5 岁）	4 月，乔伊斯一家迁居至金斯敦（Kingstown），即邓莱里（Dún Laoghaire）南部布雷（Bray）的马尔泰洛碉堡（Martello）或称圆形炮塔 1 号平台，他们在那里住到 1891 年 8 月。

	4 月，《伦敦时报》（*The London Times*）发表了该报记者理查德·皮戈特（Richard Pigott, 1838？—89）对爱尔兰自治党领袖查尔斯·斯图尔特·帕内尔（Charles Stewart Parnell, 1846—1891）的指控。
1888 年 （6 岁）	9 月，詹姆斯·乔伊斯被送到基尔代尔县（County Kildare）萨林斯（Sallins）附近的克朗戈伍斯森林公学（Clongowes Wood College），这是一家耶稣会寄宿学校。他一直在这里待到 1891 年 6 月，在这期间，他仅在假期回家。
1889 年 （7 岁）	2 月，理查德·皮戈特被揭发弄虚作假，他自己承认了作假行为。在此期间，查尔斯·斯图尔特·帕内尔在议会的政治权威达到顶峰。 3 月，理查德·皮戈特自杀。 3 月，詹姆斯·乔伊斯因使用"粗言秽语"而在学校被藤鞭抽打了 4 下。 12 月，下议院议员威廉·亨利·奥谢上尉（Captain William Henry O'Shea, 1840—1905）提出与其妻凯瑟琳·奥谢（Katherine O'Shea, 1846—1921）即凯蒂·奥谢（Katie O'Shea）或基蒂·奥谢（Kitty O'Shea）离婚，理由是她与查尔斯·斯图尔特·帕内尔通奸。 阿瑟·格里菲思（Arthur Griffith, 1872—1922）创办一份周报《联合起来的爱尔兰人》（*United Irishman*）。
1890 年 （8 岁）	查尔斯·斯图尔特·帕内尔在爱尔兰自治党内倒台。
1891 年 （9 岁）	10 月 6 日（从此以后成为"常春藤日"），"爱尔兰无冕之王"查尔斯·斯图尔特·帕内尔在布莱顿谢世。 1891 年底，詹姆斯·乔伊斯写了一首名为《还有你，希利》（*Et Tu, Healy*）的挽歌，以纪念查尔斯·斯图尔特·帕内尔并抨击曾经做过帕内尔的副手，后来成为已故英雄的死敌的蒂莫西·迈克尔·希利（Timothy Michael Healy, 1855—1931），后者亦被称作蒂姆·希利（Tim Healy）。 约翰·斯坦尼斯劳斯·乔伊斯——帕内尔的坚定的拥护者——设法出版了《还有你，希利》。但该诗的印刷稿没有一份被保存下来。 詹姆斯·乔伊斯从克朗戈伍斯森林公学退学。
1892 年 （10 岁）	乔伊斯一家移居位于都柏林市郊布莱克罗克（Blackrock）凯里斯福特大街（Carysfort avenue）23 号，他们在那里居住到同年 11 月。 詹姆斯·乔伊斯在 1892 年没有上学。 自 1892 年 11 月至 1894 年底，乔伊斯一家居住在菲茨吉本大街 14 号。 威廉·尤尔特·格拉德斯通《自治法案》又未获通过。
1893 年 （11 岁）	4 月，詹姆斯·乔伊斯开始在另一所耶稣会创办的学校贝尔韦代雷公学（Belvedere College）上学，他在那里是走读生。

盖尔联合会(the Gaelic League)由爱俄·麦克尼尔(Eoin MacNeill, Irish: *Eoin Mac Néill*,1867—1945)和道格拉斯·海德(Douglas Hyde, Irish: *Dubhghlas de hÍde*,1860—1949)创立,旨在复兴爱尔兰语和爱尔兰传统。

乔伊斯一家分别在菲茨吉本大街 14 号和哈德威克大街 29 号两处居住过。

1894 年 (12 岁)	10 月,乔伊斯一家从菲茨吉本大街 14 号迁居至庄康爪(Drumcondra)米尔伯恩大街(Millbourne Avenue)霍利韦尔别墅(Holywell Villas)2 号。

詹姆斯·乔伊斯阅读查尔斯·兰姆(Charles Lamb, 1764—1834)所著《尤利西斯历险记》(*The Adventures of Ulysses*,1808),他选择足智多谋的尤利西斯作为其最喜爱的英雄,并写了一篇名为《我最喜爱的英雄》(*My Favourite Hero*)的作文。

1895 年
(13 岁)
詹姆斯·乔伊斯参加圣母马利亚联谊会(the Sodality of the Blessed Virgin Mary)。

1896 年
(14 岁)
4 月,乔伊斯一家移居里士满北大街(North Richmond Street),在此处住到同年 11 月。

从 1896 年 9 月至 1899 年 7 月,乔伊斯一家住在费尔维尤(Fairview)温莎大街(Windsor Avenue)29 号。

9 月,詹姆斯·乔伊斯在圣母马利亚联谊会里被选举为负责人。

詹姆斯·乔伊斯遇到一个妓女,后者让他首次体验了性生活。

据信,《勿信外表》(*Trust Not Appearances*)是詹姆斯·乔伊斯在贝尔韦代雷公学求学期间每周写作练习中惟一保存下来的作文,它写于 1896 年。

1897 年
(15 岁)
1897 年春,詹姆斯·乔伊斯因考试成绩名列第 13 而获得 33 英镑奖学金。

詹姆斯·乔伊斯与其母同去礼拜。

10 月,詹姆斯·乔伊斯购买了《效法基督》(*Imitation of Christ*)一书。这被视为他最后一次对宗教的热情。

1898 年
(16 岁)
6 月,詹姆斯·乔伊斯逃避了一次宗教课考试。

7 月,詹姆斯·乔伊斯偶遇一位"像鸟一样的少女"。

詹姆斯·乔伊斯离开贝尔韦代雷公学。

9 月,詹姆斯·乔伊斯就读都柏林大学(University College Dublin)。

9 月 27 日,詹姆斯·乔伊斯写了一篇论"力"(Force)的小品文。

据信,詹姆斯·乔伊斯在 1898 年至 1899 年参加都柏林大学入学考试时撰写了题为《语言学习》(*The Study of Languages*)的杂文。

1899 年 （17 岁）	5 月，爱尔兰文学剧场（Irish Literary Theatre）开始演出威廉·巴特勒·叶芝（William Butler Yeats，1865—1939）创作的戏剧《伯爵夫人凯瑟琳》（*The Countess Cathleen*）。詹姆斯·乔伊斯当时看过演出。 自 7 月至 9 月，詹姆斯·乔伊斯在费尔维尤的修女大街（Convent Avenue）消夏。 自 1899 年 9 月至 1900 年 5 月，詹姆斯·乔伊斯居住在里士满大街（Richmond Avenue）13 号。 9 月，詹姆斯·乔伊斯写了一篇论《戴荆冠的耶稣画像》或译作《你们看这个人》（*Ecce Homo*）的杂文。 10 月，查尔斯·斯图尔特·帕内尔纪念碑基座建在都柏林萨克威尔上游大街（Upper Sackville Street）即奥康内尔大街（O'Connell Street）。
1900 年 （18 岁）	1 月 10 日，詹姆斯·乔伊斯写了一篇名为《戏剧与人生》（*Drama and Life*）的文章。 1 月 20 日，詹姆斯·乔伊斯在文学与历史协会（Literary and Historical Society）门前宣读了这篇题为《戏剧与人生》（*Drama and Life*）的讲演稿。 2 月，詹姆斯·乔伊斯观看了由乔治·摩尔（George Moore，1852—1933）和爱德华·马丁（Edward Martyn，1859—1923）合创的戏剧《折枝》（*The Bending of the Bough*，1900）。 4 月 1 日，詹姆斯·乔伊斯的评论《易卜生的新剧》（*Ibsen's New drama*）发表在《半月评论》（*Fortnightly Review*）上。该文是关于亨里克·约翰·易卜生（Henrik Johan Ibsen，1828—1906）的戏剧《当我们死而复生时》（*When We Dead Awaken*，1899）的评论，它是詹姆斯·乔伊斯第一部正式发表的作品。 4 月，詹姆斯·乔伊斯收到亨里克·约翰·易卜生的致谢信。 5 月，乔伊斯一家从里士满大街 13 号迁居至费尔维尤皇家阳台（Royal Terrace）8 号。
1901 年 （19 岁）	3 月，詹姆斯·乔伊斯向亨里克·约翰·易卜生寄去一封贺寿信。 自 1901 年 10 月至 1902 年 9 月，乔伊斯一家居住在格伦加里夫广场（Glengariff Parade）32 号。 10 月 15 日，詹姆斯·乔伊斯写了一篇名为《喧嚣的时代》（*The Day of the Rabblement*）的文章。 《喧嚣的时代》与弗朗西斯·斯凯芬顿（Francis Skeffington）的一篇散文合在一起，以《两篇散文》（*Two Essays*）为题目自费在都柏林发表。

1902 年　　2 月 15 日,詹姆斯·乔伊斯在都柏林大学的文学与历史协会里宣读
（20 岁）　　了一篇关于爱尔兰诗人詹姆斯·克拉伦斯·曼根（James Clarence Mangan, 1803—1949）的讲演稿。

10 月,詹姆斯·乔伊斯在圣塞西莉亚的一家医学院注册。

10 月,詹姆斯·乔伊斯在都柏林大学获得文学学士学位。

11 月,詹姆斯·乔伊斯的评论《一位爱尔兰诗人》（*An Irish Poet*）在都柏林《每日快报》（*Daily Express*）发表,对威廉·鲁尼（William Rooney）的作品《诗篇与民谣》（*Poems and Ballads*）作了评论。

11 月,詹姆斯·乔伊斯同威廉·巴特勒·叶芝和伊莎贝拉·奥古斯塔·格雷戈里（Isabella Augusta Gregory, 1852—1932）在拿骚酒店（Nassau Hotel）就餐。伊莎贝拉·奥古斯塔·格雷戈里亦被称作格雷戈里夫人（Lady Gregory）。

12 月 1 日,詹姆斯·乔伊斯离开都柏林去了巴黎。

12 月 11 日,詹姆斯·乔伊斯在都柏林的《每日快报》上发表评论,对沃尔特·杰罗尔德斯（Walter Jerrolds）的作品《乔治·梅雷迪斯》（*George Meredith*）作了评论。

12 月 24 日,詹姆斯·乔伊斯结识爱尔兰文艺复兴运动中的重要诗人奥利弗·圣约翰·戈加蒂（Oliver St. John Gogarty, 1878—1957）——《尤利西斯》（*Ulysses*, 1922）中巴克·马利根（Buck Mulligan）的原型。

同年末,乔伊斯一家移居圣彼得阳台（Saint Peter's Terrace）7 号。

1903 年　　1 月 29 日,詹姆斯·乔伊斯在都柏林的《每日快报》上发表文章,对
（21 岁）　　斯蒂芬·格温（Stephen Lucius Gwynn, 1864—1950）的作品《爱尔兰的今天和明天》（*Today and To-morrow in Ireland*）作了评论。

2 月 6 日,詹姆斯·乔伊斯在都柏林的《每日快报》上发表题为《温和哲学》（*A Suave Philosophy*）的文章,对菲尔丁-霍尔（Fielding-Hall）的作品《民族魂》（*The Soul of a People*）作了评论。

2 月 6 日,詹姆斯·乔伊斯在都柏林的《每日快报》上发表题为《缜思之努力》（*An Effort at Precision in Thinking*）的文章,对詹姆斯·安斯蒂（James Anstie）的作品《大众谈话》（*Colloquies of Common People*）作了评论。

2 月 6 日,詹姆斯·乔伊斯在都柏林的《每日快报》上发表题为《殖民诗》（*Colonial Verses*）的文章,对克莱夫·菲利普斯-沃利（Clive Phillips-Wolley）的作品《英国以扫之歌》（*Songs of an English Esau*）作了评论。

2 月 13 日,詹姆斯·乔伊斯在其"巴黎笔记"（*Paris Notebook*）上指出:喜剧优于悲剧。

3 月 6 日,詹姆斯·乔伊斯在其"巴黎笔记"上探讨了艺术的 3 种形式:抒情的形式、史诗的形式和戏剧的形式。

3月 21 日，詹姆斯·乔伊斯的评论发表在伦敦的《发言人》（*Speaker*）上，对亨里克·约翰·易卜生所创作的《卡蒂利纳》（*Catilina*，1850）的法译本作了评论。

3月 26 日，詹姆斯·乔伊斯在爱尔兰的《每日快报》上发表题为《爱尔兰之魂》（*The Soul of Ireland*）的评论，对格雷戈里夫人的作品《诗人与梦想家》（*Poets and Dreamers*）作了评论。

3月 28 日，詹姆斯·乔伊斯在其"巴黎笔记"上，给艺术下了定义。

4月 7 日，詹姆斯·乔伊斯在都柏林的《爱尔兰时报》（*Irish Times*）上发表了一篇题为《汽车公开赛》（*The Motor Derby*）的文章。该文的副标题为《法国冠军采访录》（*Interview with the French Champion（from a correspondent）*）。

4月 10 日，詹姆斯·乔伊斯收到父亲的电报，便返回都柏林。这份电报上写道："毋[母]病危"（NOTHER [MOTHER] DYING）。

8月 13 日，詹姆斯·乔伊斯母亲病故，他烧毁父亲给母亲的情书。

9月 3 日，詹姆斯·乔伊斯在都柏林的《每日快报》上发表评论，对约翰·伯内特（John Burnet）的作品《亚里士多德论教育》（*Aristotle on Education*）进行了评论。

9月 17 日，詹姆斯·乔伊斯在都柏林的《每日快报》上发表题为《新小说》（*New Fiction*）的评论，对阿奎拉·肯普斯特（Aquila Kempster）的作品《阿迦·米尔扎王子历险记》（*The Adventures of Prince Aga Mirza*）进行了评论。

9月 17 日，詹姆斯·乔伊斯在都柏林的《每日快报》上发表评论，对莱恩·艾伦（Lane Allen）的作品《牧场活力》（*The Mettle of the Pasture*）进行了评论。

9月 17 日，詹姆斯·乔伊斯在都柏林的《每日快报》上发表题为《窥史》（*A Peep Into History*）的评论，对约翰·波洛克（John Pollock）的作品《主教的阴谋》（*The Popish Plot*）进行了评论。

10月 1 日，詹姆斯·乔伊斯在都柏林的《每日快报》上发表题为《法国宗教小说》（*A French Religious Novel*）的评论，对玛塞尔·蒂奈尔（Marcelle Tinayre）的作品《罪之屋》（*The House of Sin*）进行了评论。

10月 1 日，詹姆斯·乔伊斯在都柏林的《每日快报》上发表题为《不压韵的诗》（*Unequal Verse*）的评论，对弗雷德里克·兰布里奇（Frederick Langbridge）的作品《民谣与传说》（*Ballads and Legend*）进行了评论。

10月 1 日，詹姆斯·乔伊斯在都柏林的《每日快报》上发表题为《阿诺德·格雷夫斯先生》（*Mr. Arnold Graves*）的评论，对阿诺德·格雷夫斯（Arnold Graves）的作品《克吕泰墨斯特拉：一场悲剧》（*Clytoemnestra：A Tragedy*）进行了评论。

10月15日,詹姆斯·乔伊斯在都柏林的《每日快报》上发表题为《被忽视的诗人》(*A Neglected Poet*)的评论,对艾尔弗雷德·安杰(Alfred Ainger)的作品《乔治·格拉贝》(*George Grabbe*)进行了评论。

10月15日,詹姆斯·乔伊斯在都柏林的《每日快报》上发表题为《梅森先生的小说》(*Mr. Mason's Novels*)的评论,对艾尔弗雷德·爱德华·伍德利·梅森(Alfred Edward Woodley Mason,1865—1948)的小说进行了评论。

10月30日,詹姆斯·乔伊斯在都柏林的《每日快报》上发表题为《布鲁诺哲学》(*The Bruno Philosophy*)的评论,对 J. 刘易斯·麦金太尔(J. Lewis McIntyre)的作品《乔达诺·布鲁诺》(*Giordano Bruno*)进行了评论。

11月12日,詹姆斯·乔伊斯在都柏林的《每日快报》上发表题为《人道主义》(*Humanism*)的评论,对费迪南·坎宁·斯科特·席勒(Ferdinand Canning Scott Schiller,1864—1937)的作品《人道主义:哲学随笔》(*Humanism：Philosophical Essays*)进行了评论。

11月12日,詹姆斯·乔伊斯在都柏林的《每日快报》上发表题为《讲解莎士比亚》(*Shakespeare Explained*)的评论,对 A. S. 坎宁(A. S. Canning)的作品《莎士比亚八剧研究》(*Shakespeare Studied in Eight Plays*)进行了评论。

11月26日,詹姆斯·乔伊斯在都柏林的《每日快报》上发表文章,对 T. 巴伦·拉塞尔(T. Baron Russell)的作品《博莱斯父子》(*Borlase and Son*)进行了评论。

1904 年 (22 岁)	1月,詹姆斯·乔伊斯开始撰写《斯蒂芬英雄》(*Stephen Hero*,1944)。此书是《艺术家年轻时的写照》(*A Portrait of the Artist as a Young Man*,1916)初稿的一部分。1944 年版的《斯蒂芬英雄》由西奥多·斯潘塞(Theodore Spencer,1902—1949)校订,由纽约的新方向出版社和伦敦的乔纳森·凯普出版社出版。 2月,詹姆斯·乔伊斯创作完《斯蒂芬英雄》的第一章。 这年春天,詹姆斯·乔伊斯在多基(Dalkey)的克利夫顿学校(Clifton School)获得授课之职,他在那里一直待到同年 6 月底。 5月,詹姆斯·乔伊斯参加了"爱尔兰音乐节"(Feis Ceoil)歌咏赛。此音乐节是每年一次的爱尔兰艺术节。詹姆斯·乔伊斯在歌咏赛上获得三等奖,得到铜质奖章。 大约在 6 月 10 日,詹姆斯·乔伊斯遇到一位名叫诺拉·巴那克尔(Nora Barnacle,1884—1951)的戈尔韦(Galway)女孩。该女子当时正在都柏林的芬恩旅馆(Finn's Hotel)工作。

| 乔伊斯作品中的
凯尔特歌谣

也许,在6月16日——布卢姆日(Bloomsday)——詹姆斯·乔伊斯与诺拉·巴那克尔约会。正是这一日被詹姆斯·乔伊斯选为小说《尤利西斯》的故事发生日。

7月,詹姆斯·乔伊斯创作完短篇小说《姐俩》或译作《姐妹们》(The Sisters),并为此领到一沙弗林(sovereign)稿费。

8月13日,詹姆斯·乔伊斯创作的短篇小说《姐俩》在A. E.或Æ即乔治·威廉·拉塞尔(George William Russell,1867—1935)任编辑的报纸《爱尔兰家园》(TheIrish Homestead)上发表。詹姆斯·乔伊斯发表这篇作品时,采用的笔名是斯蒂芬·代达罗斯。

9月,詹姆斯·乔伊斯住在桑迪湾马尔泰洛碉堡(Sandycove Martello Tower)。此处由奥利弗·戈加蒂租下。在这里与詹姆斯·乔伊斯一起住的有奥利弗·戈加蒂和塞缪尔·特伦奇(Samuel Trench)。

9月10日,詹姆斯·乔伊斯创作的《伊芙琳》(Eveline)在《爱尔兰家园》上发表。

10月8日,詹姆斯·乔伊斯和诺拉·巴那克尔离开都柏林,前往瑞士东北部城市苏黎世。他在1904年离开都柏林前大约2个月,创作了一首讽刺诗《宗教法庭》(The Holy Office)。

10月20日,詹姆斯·乔伊斯和诺拉·巴那克尔到达的里雅斯特(Trieste)——意大利东北部港市。

10月21日,詹姆斯·乔伊斯和诺拉·巴那克尔到达普拉镇(Pola或Pula)。

11月7日,詹姆斯·乔伊斯在其"普拉笔记"中主张善、真、美(the good,the true,and the beautiful)三合一。

11月15日,詹姆斯·乔伊斯在其"普拉笔记"中引用中世纪意大利经院哲学家圣托马斯·阿奎那(Saint Thomas Aquinas,1225—74)的语句讨论美。

11月16日,詹姆斯·乔伊斯在其"普拉笔记"中讨论"理解的行为"(the act of apprehension)。

11月,詹姆斯·乔伊斯开始创作短篇小说《泥土》(Clay),直至1906年底才写完,它与《都柏林人》的其它短篇小说集合在了一起,在1914年发表。

12月17日,詹姆斯·乔伊斯的短篇小说《车赛之后》(After the Race)在《爱尔兰家园》上发表。

12月,由爱尔兰国家戏剧协会(Irish National Theatre Society)在都柏林筹建的阿比剧院(Abbey Theatre)开始公演。

1905年
(23岁)

自1月至3月,詹姆斯·乔伊斯住在奥地利普拉镇维亚梅蒂诺路(Via Medolino)7号。

3月,詹姆斯·乔伊斯到的里雅斯特市伯利兹学校任课。

自3月至5月,詹姆斯·乔伊斯住在的里雅斯特市蓬泰偌索广场(Piazza Ponterosso)3号。

自1905年5月至1906年2月,詹姆斯·乔伊斯住在的里雅斯特市维亚圣尼古拉路(Via S Nicolò)30号。

7月,詹姆斯·乔伊斯创作了短篇小说《寄寓》(*The Boarding House*)。该作品最早作为《都柏林人》的一篇故事,于1914年发表。

7月,詹姆斯·乔伊斯创作了短篇小说《对手》(*Counterparts*)。该作品最初发表于1914年。

7月,詹姆斯·乔伊斯的短篇小说《悲痛的往事》(*A Painful Case*)做了几次修改,它最早作为《都柏林人》的一篇故事,于1914年发表。

7月27日,詹姆斯·乔伊斯的儿子乔治亚·乔伊斯(Giorgio Joyce)出生。

詹姆斯·乔伊斯的短篇小说《委员会办公室里的常春藤日》(*Ivy Day in the Committee Room*)在1905年夏写完,它最初发表于1914年。

9月,詹姆斯·乔伊斯的短篇小说《偶遇》(*An Encounter*)写完,它被收入第一版《都柏林人》中。

9月底,詹姆斯·乔伊斯的短篇小说《母亲》(*A Mother*)写完,它最初作为《都柏林人》的一篇故事,于1914年发表。

10月中旬,詹姆斯·乔伊斯的短篇小说《阿拉比》(*Araby*)写完,它最初发表于1914年。

詹姆斯·乔伊斯的短篇小说《圣恩》(*Grace*)大部分写于1905年,部分修改于1906年,该作最初发表于1914年。

10月20日,斯坦尼斯劳斯·乔伊斯离开都柏林,来到的里雅斯特,与詹姆斯·乔伊斯一家住在一起。

11月,新芬党(Sinn Féin party)创立。在爱尔兰语中,"Sinn Féin"表示"我们自己"(ourselves 或 we ourselves),但常被误译作"只有我们自己"(ourselves alone)。

12月,詹姆斯·乔伊斯把由12篇短篇小说组成的《都柏林人》交给出版商格兰特·理查兹(Grant Richards)。

詹姆斯·乔伊斯的诗歌《宗教法庭》自费出版。

1906年 (24岁)	2月,乔伊斯一家住进薄伽丘路(Via Giovanni Boccaccio)的一幢公寓。 7月,詹姆斯·乔伊斯带诺拉·巴那克尔和乔治亚·乔伊斯到达罗马。 8月,詹姆斯·乔伊斯开始在纳斯特-科尔布和舒马赫(Nast-Kolb & Schumacher)银行作职员。 9月,乔伊斯一家迁至另一公寓,该公寓位于维亚蒙特布里安丘山路(Via Monte Brianzo)。

詹姆斯·乔伊斯完成了短篇小说《两个浪子》（*Two Gallants*）的创作，该作品最初发表于 1914 年。

詹姆斯·乔伊斯的短篇小说《一小片云》（*A Little Cloud*）写完，它最初发表于 1914 年。

1907 年 （25 岁）	1 月 17 日，詹姆斯·乔伊斯与埃尔金·马修斯出版社（Elkin Matthews）签下出版诗集《室内乐》（*Chamber Music*，1907）的合同。 3 月 7 日，詹姆斯·乔伊斯一家回到的里雅斯特。 3 月 22 日，詹姆斯·乔伊斯用意大利文撰写的评论《女性主义：最后的芬尼亚勇士》（*Il Fenianismo. L'Ultimo feniano*）在的里雅斯特的《晚邮报》（*Il Piccolo della Sera*）上发表。 4 月 27 日，詹姆斯·乔伊斯在的里雅斯特民众大学（Università Popolare Triestina）用意大利文做了一个题为《爱尔兰，圣贤之岛》（*Irlanda，Isola dei Santi e dei Savi*）的讲演。 5 月 10 日，詹姆斯·乔伊斯的诗集《室内乐》在伦敦由埃尔金·马修斯出版社出版。 5 月 19 日，詹姆斯·乔伊斯用意大利文撰写的评论《自治法案进入成熟期》（*Home Rule Maggiorenne*）在的里雅斯特的《晚邮报》上发表。 7 月 26 日是圣安妮节（St Anne's day），詹姆斯·乔伊斯的女儿露西娅·安娜·乔伊斯（Lucia Anna Joyce）出生。 9 月 16 日，詹姆斯·乔伊斯用意大利文撰写的评论《公审中的爱尔兰》（*L'Irland alla Sbarra*）在的里雅斯特的《晚邮报》上发表。 在 1907 年，詹姆斯·乔伊斯的短篇小说《死者》写于的里雅斯特，该作最早作为《都柏林人》的一篇故事，于 1914 年发表。
1908 年 （26 岁）	詹姆斯·乔伊斯写完《艺术家年轻时的写照》前 3 章。
1909 年 （27 岁）	3 月 24 日，詹姆斯·乔伊斯用意大利文撰写的评论《奥斯卡·王尔德：〈莎乐美〉的诗人作者》（*Oscar Wilde：Il Poeta di 'Salome'*）在的里雅斯特的《晚邮报》上发表。 4 月，詹姆斯·乔伊斯修改过的《都柏林人》被送到都柏林的蒙塞尔出版公司（Maunsel & Company）。 8 月 6 日，文森特·科斯格罗夫（Vincent Cosgrave）——《艺术家年轻时的写照》中林奇（Lynch）的原型——断言诺拉·巴那克尔背叛过詹姆斯·乔伊斯。 8 月 7 日，詹姆斯·乔伊斯找住在埃克尔斯街 7 号的老朋友 J. F. 伯恩（J. F. Byrne）——《艺术家年轻时的写照》中克兰利（Cranly）的原型——帮忙。埃克尔斯街 7 号是《尤利西斯》主角利奥波德·布卢姆（Leopold Bloom）的家。 8 月，詹姆斯·乔伊斯带着儿子乔治亚·乔伊斯回到爱尔兰。

8月31日,乔治亚·乔伊斯在都柏林用意大利文写了一篇文章,该文题目为《萧伯纳与审查员的交锋:布兰科·波斯内特的出现》(*La Battaglia Fra Bernard Shaw e la Censura.* "*Blanco Posnet Smascherato*")。

9月5日,詹姆斯·乔伊斯用意大利文撰写的文章《萧伯纳与审查员的交锋:布兰科·波斯内特的出现》在的里雅斯特的《晚邮报》上发表。

9月9日,詹姆斯·乔伊斯带着儿子乔治亚·乔伊斯以及妹妹伊娃·乔伊斯(Eva Joyce)回到的里雅斯特。

10月21日,詹姆斯·乔伊斯回到都柏林。

12月20日,詹姆斯·乔伊斯开设的沃尔特电影院(Cinematographic Volta)开始营业。

詹姆斯·乔伊斯送给妻子一条项链,它上面刻着:"爱之离,爱则悲。"(Love is unhappy when love is away.)

1910年 (28岁)	1月,詹姆斯·乔伊斯回到的里雅斯特。 6月,沃尔特电影院被卖掉,赔600英镑。 12月22日,詹姆斯·乔伊斯用意大利文撰写的文章《自治法案彗星》(*La Cometa dell* "*Home Rule*")在的里雅斯特的《晚邮报》上发表。
1912年 (30岁)	3月,詹姆斯·乔伊斯用意大利文在的里雅斯特民众大学做了一个关于威廉·布莱克(William Blake, 1757—1827)的讲演。 5月16日,詹姆斯·乔伊斯用意大利文撰写的文章《忆帕内尔》(*L'Ombra di Parnell*)在的里雅斯特的《晚邮报》上发表。 自7月至9月,詹姆斯·乔伊斯回爱尔兰办事,此行是他最后一次回爱尔兰。期间,他到过戈尔韦(Galway)和都柏林。 8月11日,詹姆斯·乔伊斯用意大利文撰写的文章《部落城市:意大利语在爱尔兰港回荡》(*La Città delle Tribù; Ricordi Italiani in un Porto Irlandese*)在的里雅斯特的《晚邮报》上发表。 8月23日,都柏林的蒙塞尔出版公司(Maunsel & Company)拒绝出版《都柏林人》。 9月5日,詹姆斯·乔伊斯用意大利文撰写的文章《阿兰岛渔夫的幻想:发生战争时英格兰的安全阀》(*Il Miraggio del Pescatore di Aran. La Valvola dell'Inghilterra in Caso di Guerra*)在的里雅斯特的《晚邮报》上发表。 9月10日,詹姆斯·乔伊斯的文章《政治与牛疫》(*Politics and Cattle Disease*)在《自由人杂志》(*Freeman's Journal*)上发表。 9月,詹姆斯·乔伊斯的讽刺诗《火炉冒出的煤气》(*Gas from a Burner*)在的里雅斯特自费出版。

1913 年 （31 岁）	詹姆斯·乔伊斯经威廉·巴特勒·叶芝介绍，与艾兹拉·庞德（Ezra Pound，1885—1972）交往。
	詹姆斯·乔伊斯开始为创作剧本《流亡者》(*Exiles*，1918)做笔记。
1914 年 （32 岁）	2 月，詹姆斯·乔伊斯的小说《艺术家年轻时的写照》在伦敦杂志《自我主义者》(*Egoist*)上分期发表。
	3 月，詹姆斯·乔伊斯开始写小说《尤利西斯》，但又暂时停下《尤利西斯》的创作，以便撰写《流亡者》。《流亡者》于 1915 年写完。
	6 月 15 日，詹姆斯·乔伊斯短篇小说集《都柏林人》由伦敦格兰特·理查兹有限公司(Grant Richards Ltd)出版。
	7 月 15 日，《〈都柏林人〉与詹姆斯·乔伊斯先生》(*Dublinersand Mr. James Joyce*)——艾兹拉·庞德关于《都柏林人》的评论在《自我主义者》上发表。
1915 年 （33 岁）	4 月，詹姆斯·乔伊斯离开的里雅斯特去瑞士。
	6 月，詹姆斯·乔伊斯一家到达苏黎世。
	8 月，在艾兹拉·庞德、埃德蒙·戈斯(Edmund Gosse，1849—1928)和威廉·巴特勒·叶芝的帮助下，詹姆斯·乔伊斯获得一笔由不列颠皇家文学基金会(British Royal Literary Fund)颁发的资金。
	9 月，詹姆斯·乔伊斯写完剧本《流亡者》。
1916 年 （34 岁）	9 月，詹姆斯·乔伊斯收到不列颠国库基金(British Treasury Fund)赠予的 100 英镑。
	12 月 29 日，詹姆斯·乔伊斯的小说《艺术家年轻时的写照》由纽约的 B. W. 许布希出版社(B. W. Huebsch)出版。
	伦敦自我主义者出版社(Egoist Press)出版《艺术家年轻时的写照》。
	纽约的现代书屋(Modern Library)出版《都柏林人》。
	《都柏林人》一个版本由纽约的 B. W. 许布希出版社出版。
	詹姆斯·乔伊斯创作了一首题为《杜利的谨慎》(*Dooleysprudence*)的诗。
1917 年 （35 岁）	2 月，《小说终于出现》(*At last the Novel Appears*)——艾兹拉·庞德关于《艺术家年轻时的写照》的评论在《自我主义者》上发表。
	4 月 1 日，詹姆斯·乔伊斯在 B. W. 许布希出版社出版的《艺术家年轻时的写照》中校出 365 处错误。
	4 月 24 日，复活节起义(Easter Rebellion)主要发生在都柏林。
	8 月，艾兹拉·庞德撰写的《詹姆斯·乔伊斯的长篇小说》(*James Joyce's Novel*)在《小评论》(*Little Review*)上发表。
	8 月，詹姆斯·乔伊斯做了眼部手术。
	10 月，为了康复，詹姆斯·乔伊斯去瑞士南部洛迦诺(Locarno)疗养。
	哈里特·肖·韦弗(Harriet Shaw Weaver，1876—1961)——《自我主义者》杂志的编辑——开始匿名资助詹姆斯·乔伊斯。

埃蒙·德·瓦勒拉(Éamon de Valera，1882—1975)被选为新芬党主席。

1916 年版的《艺术家年轻时的写照》由自我主义者出版社重印。

詹姆斯·休谟克(James Huneker，1857—1921)的评论《詹姆斯·乔伊斯》被收入斯克里布纳出版社（Scribner）出版的《独角兽》(Unicorns，1917)中。

1918 年 （36 岁）	1 月，詹姆斯·乔伊斯回到苏黎世。

2 月，詹姆斯·乔伊斯翻译的迭戈·安杰利(Diego Angeli)的评论《论〈写照〉的意大利书评》(Un Romanzo di Gesuiti)在《自我主义者》上发表。

3 月，长篇小说《尤利西斯》第一章由纽约《小评论》发表。

1918 年，《尤利西斯》如下各章先后在《小评论》上发表：

3 月，《忒勒马科斯》(Telemachus)；

4 月，《涅斯托耳》(Nestor)；

5 月，《普洛透斯》(Proteus)；

6 月，《卡吕普索》(Calypso)；

7 月，《食莲者》(Lotus eaters)；

9 月，《冥府》(Hades)；

10 月，《埃俄罗斯》(Eolus)。

5 月，詹姆斯·乔伊斯的《流亡者》由伦敦格兰特·理查兹有限公司出版。

1919 年 （37 岁）	1 月，爱尔兰议会第一次会议召开。

10 月，詹姆斯·乔伊斯和其家人返回的里雅斯特。

1919 年，《尤利西斯》如下各章先后在《小评论》上发表：

1 月和 2 月/3 月，《勒斯特里冈尼亚人》(Lestrygonians)；

4 月和 5 月，《斯库拉与卡律布狄斯》(Scylla and Charybdis)；

6 月和 7 月，《游岩》(Wandering Rocks)；

8 月和 9 月，《赛壬》(Sirens)；

11 月和 12 月，《独眼巨人》(Cyclops)一部分。

4 月 10 日，英国女作家弗吉尼亚·吴尔夫(Virginia Woolf，1882—1941)的《现代长篇小说》(Modern Novels)在《时代文学供给》(Times Literary Supply)发表。她在此文中赞赏了詹姆斯·乔伊斯叙事技巧的原创性。1925 年，《现代长篇小说》改题为《现代小说》(Modern Fiction)，刊登在《普通读者》(The Common Reader)上。

6 月，由一位匿名作者撰写的题为《与新小说共超巅峰》(Over the Top with the New Novelists)的文章发表在《时事评论》(Current Opinion)上，该文对连载中的《尤利西斯》和《艺术家年轻时的写照》进行了评论，文中大量征引了弗吉尼亚·吴尔夫的《现代长篇小说》的语句。

| 1920 年 | 6 月,詹姆斯·乔伊斯带其子乔治亚·乔伊斯到意大利的代森扎诺- |
| (38 岁) | 德尔加达(Desenzano del Garda)与艾兹拉·庞德会晤。 |

1920 年
(38 岁)

6 月,詹姆斯·乔伊斯带其子乔治亚·乔伊斯到意大利的代森扎诺-德尔加达(Desenzano del Garda)与艾兹拉·庞德会晤。

6 月,詹姆斯·乔伊斯在艾兹拉·庞德的建议下,携带家人迁居巴黎。

1920 年,《尤利西斯》如下各章先后在《小评论》上发表:

1 月和 2 月,《独眼巨人》(Cyclops)剩余部分;

4 月,5 月/6 月和 7 月/8 月,《瑙西卡》(Nausikaa);

9 月/12 月,《太阳神的牛》(Oxen of the Sun)。

8 月,经艾兹拉·庞德介绍,詹姆斯·乔伊斯结识托马斯·斯特恩斯·艾略特(Thomas Stearns Eliot, 1888—1965)。

9 月 3 日,詹姆斯·乔伊斯给约翰·奎因(John Quinn)写了一封信,信中有一份《尤利西斯》纲要。

1921 年
(39 岁)

2 月,查尔斯·斯图尔特·帕内尔的情人和妻子凯瑟琳·奥谢·帕内尔谢世。

2 月,《小评论》因有淫秽嫌疑而开始受审,纽约法庭判定《尤利西斯》会伤风败俗。

4 月,理查德·奥尔丁顿(Richard Aldington)撰写的《詹姆斯·乔伊斯先生的影响》(The Influence of Mr. James Joyce)在《英语评论》(The English Review)上发表。

6 月 11 日,萧伯纳或直译为乔治·伯纳德·肖(George Bernard Shaw, 1856—1950)给出版家西尔维娅·比奇(Sylvia Beach, 1887—1962)写了一封信,表达了他对连载的《尤利西斯》的看法。

8 月 16 日,詹姆斯·乔伊斯写信给其友人弗兰克·巴奇恩(Frank Budgen, 1882—1971),告诉对方:《珀涅罗珀》(Penelope)是《尤利西斯》中最吸引人的部分。

10 月,历时 7 年,詹姆斯·乔伊斯终于撰写完《尤利西斯》,他把该书视为"两个民族(犹太-爱尔兰)的史诗"(an epic of two races (Israelite-Irish))。

12 月,爱尔兰自由邦(Irish Free State)诞生。

《流亡者》的一个版本在伦敦的自我主义者出版社出版。

詹姆斯·乔伊斯的一幅画像由温德姆·刘易斯(Wyndham Lewis)完成。

1922 年
(40 岁)

1 月,《詹姆斯·乔伊斯与居谢》(James Joyce et Pécuchet)——艾兹拉·庞德关于《尤利西斯》的一篇评论文章——在《法国信使》(Mercure de France)上发表。

1 月,亚瑟·格里菲斯(Arthur Griffith, 1871—1922)被选举为爱尔兰下议院议长。

2 月 2 日是乔伊斯 40 岁生日。这天,西尔维娅·比奇的书店即巴黎莎士比亚书屋(Shakespeare and Company)出版了《尤利西斯》第一版(共计 1000 册)。

2月11日,詹姆斯·乔伊斯给罗伯特·麦卡蒙(Robert McAlmon)写了一封信,信中提到爱尔兰下议院宣传部有意推举他为诺贝尔奖候选人,他认为自己获此奖的希望渺茫。

4月1日,《尤利西斯》(*Ulysses*)——乔治·雷姆(George Rehm)撰写的评论——在《巴黎评论》(*Paris Review*)上发表。

4月,《詹姆斯·乔伊斯》(*James Joyce*)——杜娜·巴尼斯(Djuna Barnes)撰写的评论——在《名利场》(*Vanity Fair*)上发表。

4月,詹姆斯·乔伊斯的眼疾复发。

6月,爱尔兰内战(Irish Civil War)爆发。

7月,詹姆斯·乔伊斯给艾德蒙·威尔逊(Edmund Wilson)写了一封信,对他在《新共和》(*New Republic*)和《夕阳》(*Evening Sun*)上发表的有关《尤利西斯》的评论表示欣赏。

10月,乔伊斯一家到英格兰旅游,在那里,詹姆斯·乔伊斯第一次见到哈里特·肖·韦弗。

10月,自我主义者出版社出版《尤利西斯》(共计2000册),该版中的500册被纽约邮政局(New York Post Office Authorities)扣留。

12月2日,《论尤利西斯》(On *Ulysses*)——芭贝特·德意志(Babette Deutsch)的评论——在《文学评论》(*Literary Review*)上发表。

《詹姆斯·乔伊斯的〈尤利西斯〉》(l'*Ulisse du James Joyce*)——西尔维奥·本科(Silvio Benco)的评论——在《民族报》(*La Nazione*)上发表。

爱尔兰语成为官方语言。

1923年 (41岁)	1月,伦敦的自我主义者出版社出版《尤利西斯》(共计500册,其中490册被福克斯通海关局(Customs Authorities in Folkestone)扣留。 3月,詹姆斯·乔伊斯开始创作其另一部实验性作品《进行中的工作》(*Work in Progress*)。该作品最终以《为芬尼根守灵》(*Finnegans Wake*)为题,于1939年发表。 5月,爱尔兰内战结束。 9月,爱尔兰自由邦被允许加入国际联盟(League of Nations)。 10月23日,詹姆斯·乔伊斯给哈里特·肖·韦弗写了一封信,他在信中提到中国女士和上海。 11月14日,威廉·巴特勒·叶芝获诺贝尔文学奖。 11月,托马斯·斯特恩斯·艾略特的评论《〈尤利西斯〉,秩序和神话》(*Ulysses*,*Order*,*and Myth*)在《日晷》(*Dial*)上发表。 《爱尔兰反律法主义者中最新的文学信徒:詹姆斯·乔伊斯》(*Ireland's Latest Literary Antinomian*:*James Joyce*)——约瑟夫·柯林斯(Joseph Collins)撰写的文章——被收入纽约乔治·H. 多兰出版社出版的著作《神学者看文学》(*The Doctor Looks at Literature*,1923)中。《神学者看文学》的作者是约瑟夫·柯林斯本人。

1924 年 （42 岁）	1 月，莎士比亚书屋在巴黎出版了无限量版《尤利西斯》(1926 年重新排版)。
	4 月 6 日，杰拉德·古尔德(Gerald Gould)撰写的文章《论大卫·赫伯特·劳伦斯和詹姆斯·乔伊斯》(*On D. H. Lawrence and James Joyce*)在《观察者》(*Observer*)上发表。
	4 月，詹姆斯·乔伊斯《进行中的工作》的一部分在巴黎《大西洋评论》(*Transatlantic Review*)上发表。
	7 月，马尔科姆·考利(Malcolm Cowley)的文章《詹姆斯·乔伊斯》(*James Joyce*)在纽约的《文人》(*The Bookman*)上发表。
	自 7 月至 8 月中旬，詹姆斯·乔伊斯及其家人在法国圣马洛市(Saint Malo)和坎佩尔市(Quimper)度过。
	8 月 7 日，斯坦尼斯劳斯·乔伊斯给詹姆斯·乔伊斯写了一封信，信中把他哥哥尚未命名的小说(即《为芬尼根守灵》)视作"梦魇之作"(nightmare production)。
	9 月初，乔伊斯一家回到巴黎。
	11 月，艾德蒙·威尔逊的文章《走进乔伊斯》(*An Introduction to Joyce*)在《日晷》上发表。
	9 月下旬，乔伊斯一家到伦敦住了几周。
	伦敦的乔纳森·开普出版社(Jonathan Cape)出版《艺术家年轻时的写照》。
	赫伯特·戈尔曼(Herbert Gorman)的《詹姆斯·乔伊斯的早期四十年》(*James Joyce, His First Forty Years*)在纽约的 B. W. 许布希出版社出版。
	理查德·奥尔丁顿(Richard Aldington)的文章《乔伊斯先生的〈尤利西斯〉》(*Mr. James Joyce's 'Ulysses'*)被收入纽约日晷出版社出版的《文学研究和评论》(*Literary Studies and Reviews*)中。
1925 年 （43 岁）	1 月，瓦莱里·拉尔博(Valéry Larbaud，1881—1957)的文章《关于詹姆斯·乔伊斯和〈尤利西斯〉》(*A Propos de James Joyce et de Ulysses*)在《新法国评论》(*Nouvelle Revue Française*)上发表。
	3 月 13 日，詹姆斯·乔伊斯在巴黎夏尔·皮凯大道(Avenue Charles Picquet)8 号写了一封信，信中论及艾兹拉·庞德。
	3 月 14 日，西蒙娜·泰里(Simone Tery)的评论《与爱尔兰的詹姆斯·乔伊斯会晤》(*Rencontre avec Javmes Joyce, Irlandais*)在《文学新闻》(*Les Nouvelles litteraires*)上发表。
	3 月，埃内斯特·博伊德(Ernest Boyd)的评论《关于尤利西斯》(*A Propos de Ulysses*)在《新法国评论》上发表。
	4 月 4 日，伯纳德·吉尔伯特(Bernard Gilbert)的文章《詹姆斯·乔伊斯的悲剧》(*The Tragedy of James Joyce*)在《G. K. 周刊》(*G. K.'s Weekly*)上发表。

1925 年春,詹姆斯·乔伊斯那封论及艾兹拉·庞德的书信在巴黎的《本季度》(*This Quarter*)上发表。

7 月,《进行中的工作》的第二片段在伦敦的《标准》(*Criterion*)上发表。

7 月,詹姆斯·乔伊斯在法国费康(Fécamp)度过。

8 月 20 日,卡洛·利纳蒂(Carlo Linati)的文章《乔伊斯》(*Joyce*)在《晚邮报》(*Corriere della Sera*)上发表。

8 月,詹姆斯·乔伊斯在法国阿尔卡雄(Arcachon)度过。

9 月初,詹姆斯·乔伊斯回到巴黎。

9 月 12 日,詹姆斯·奥赖利(James O'Reilly)的文章《乔伊斯及他人》(Joyce and Beyond Joyce)在《爱尔兰政治家》(*Irish Statesman*)上发表。

10 月,约翰·帕尔默(John Palmer)的文章《荒诞文学》(*Antic Literature*)在《十九世纪及以后》(*Nineteenth Century and After*)上发表。

保罗·罗森菲尔德(Paul Rosenfeld)的文章《詹姆斯·乔伊斯》(*James Joyce*)被收入由纽约日暑出版社出版的《所见之人》(*Men Seen*,1925)上。

1926 年 (44 岁)	自 7 月下旬至 9 月,乔伊斯一家在奥斯坦德(Ostend)和布鲁塞尔(Brussels)度过。 9 月 19 日,欧金尼奥·蒙塔莱(Eugenio Montale)的文章《外国文学报道:詹姆斯·乔伊斯的都柏林》(*Cronache delle Letterature Straniere:Dubliners di James Joyce*)在《文学展望》(*Fiera Letteraria*)上发表。 9 月下旬,詹姆斯·乔伊斯带家人游览滑铁卢。 11 月 15 日,艾兹拉·庞德给詹姆斯·乔伊斯写了一封信,信中论及《进行中的工作》。 纽约的现代书屋出版《都柏林人》。 1924 年,乔纳森·开普出版社再版了《艺术家年轻时的写照》。
1927 年 (45 岁)	3 月 2 日,詹姆斯·乔伊斯给哈里特·肖·韦弗写了一封信,信中对一个汉字进行了讨论。 4 月,詹姆斯·乔伊斯到伦敦。 5 月和 6 月,詹姆斯·乔伊斯暂居在海牙和阿姆斯特丹。 6 月,《进行中的工作》开始在巴黎《变迁》(*transition*)上连载。 7 月,詹姆斯·乔伊斯第二本诗集《一分钱一只的果子》(*Pomes Penyeach*)在巴黎西尔维娅·比奇的莎士比亚书屋出版。 9 月,塞缪尔·罗斯(Samuel Roth)的文章《献给詹姆斯·乔伊斯》(*An Offer to James Joyce*)在《双界月刊》(*Two Worlds Monthly*)上发表。 10 月 28 日,詹姆斯·乔伊斯给哈里特·肖·韦弗写了一封信。

保罗·乔丹·史密斯(Paul Jordan Smith)的文章《打开詹姆斯·乔伊斯的〈尤利西斯〉大门的钥匙》(*A Key to the "Ulysses" of James Joyce*)在芝加哥发表。

| 1928 年
(46 岁) | 2 月 10 日,詹姆斯·乔伊斯在巴黎写了一封法文信论及托马斯·哈代(Thomas Hardy,1892—1957)。 |

1928 年第一季度,詹姆斯·乔伊斯论及托马斯·哈代的法文信在巴黎《新评论》(*Review Nouvelle*)上发表。

3 月,詹姆斯·乔伊斯到法国的迪拜(Dieppe)和鲁昂(Rouen)。

4 月下旬,詹姆斯·乔伊斯在法国的土伦(Toulon)度过。

1928 年夏,莱斯特·沙夫(Lester Scharaf)的文章《不受控制的詹姆斯·乔伊斯》(*James Joyce the Unbounded*)在巴尔的摩的《青少年》(*The Adolescent*)上发表。

自 7 月至 9 月中旬,詹姆斯·乔伊斯居住在萨尔茨堡(Salzburg)。

10 月 20 日,詹姆斯·乔伊斯创作的《安娜·利维娅·普卢拉贝勒》(*Anna Livia Plurabelle*)以著作形式在纽约发表。

12 月 29 日,A.E.(乔治·威廉·拉塞尔)的评论《安娜·利维娅·普卢拉贝勒》(*Anna Livia Plurabelle*)发表在《爱尔兰政治家》上。

乔纳森·开普出版社再版了该社于 1924 年出版的《艺术家年轻时的写照》。

纽约的兰登书屋出版了由赫伯特·戈尔曼作序的《艺术家年轻时的写照》。

| 1929 年
(47 岁) | 2 月法译本《尤利西斯》出版。 |

5 月,塞缪尔·贝克特(Samuel Beckett,1906—89)及其他 11 位作家合著的《我们对他创作的〈进行中的工作〉成果的细查》(*Our Exagmination round His Factification for Incamination of His Work in Progress*)由巴黎莎士比亚书屋出版。

卡尔·图霍斯基(Karl Tuchoisky)的评论《尤利西斯》(*Ulysses*)在《世界舞台》(*Die Weltbühne*)第二十三期(1929 年)上发表。

7 月,斯图尔特·吉伯特(Stuart Gilbert,1883—1969)的评论《爱尔兰〈尤利西斯〉一章:"冥府"》(*Irish Ulysses:Hades Episode*)在《半月评论》上发表。

8 月,詹姆斯·乔伊斯创作的《舍姆和肖恩的故事》(*Tales Told of Shem and Shaun*)由巴黎黑太阳出版社(The Black Sun Press)出版。

11 月,斯图尔特·吉伯特的评论《〈尤利西斯〉之"埃俄罗斯"》(*The Aeolus Episode of Ulysses*)在《变迁》上发表。

1929年秋,哈罗德·塞勒姆逊(Harold Salemson)的评论《詹姆斯·乔伊斯和新世界》(*James Joyce and the New World*)在巴尔的摩的《现代季刊》(*Modern Quarterly*)上发表。

10月16日,莫瑞斯·墨菲(Maurice Murphy)的评论《詹姆斯·乔伊斯和爱尔兰》(*James Joyce and Ireland*)在《民族》(*Nation*)上发表。

11月22日,詹姆斯·乔伊斯写信给哈里特·肖·韦弗,说:在过去的3周,他无法思考、写作、阅读或讲话,他每天睡眠长达16小时。

康斯坦丁·布兰库希(Constantin Brâncu i,1876—1957)的画像《乔伊斯符号》(Symbol of Joyce)发表。

彼得·杰克(Peter Jack)的评论《当代人名人:詹姆斯·乔伊斯》(*Some Contemporaries*:*James Joyce*)在《手稿》(*Manuscripts*)上发表。

1930年 (48岁)	1月,詹姆斯·乔伊斯开始力捧爱-法男高音歌手约翰·沙利文(John Sullivan),他对沙利文的支持持续了多年。 3月,斯图尔特·吉伯特的评论《普洛透斯:〈尤利西斯〉》(*Proteus*:*Ulysses*)在《交流》(*Echanges*)上发表。 5月和6月,詹姆斯·乔伊斯的左眼在苏黎世接受了一系列手术治疗。 4月23日,J. A.哈默顿(J. A. Hammerton)的评论《文学展示:我眼中的詹姆斯·乔伊斯》(*The Literary Show*:*What I think of James Joyce*)在《旁观者》(*Bystander*)上发表。 6月11日,F. B.卡基基(F. B. Cargeege)的评论《詹姆斯·乔伊斯的秘密》(*The Mystery of James Joyce*)在《普通人》(*Everyman*)上发表。 6月14日,杰拉德·赫德(Gerald Heard)的评论《詹姆斯·乔伊斯的语言》(*The Language of James Joyce*)在《周末》(*The Week-end*)上发表。 7月9日,杰斐佛·考特尼(Jeffifer Courtenay)的评论《走近詹姆斯·乔伊斯》(*The Approach to James Joyce*)在《普通人》上发表。 7月9日,G. 维内·拉斯顿(G. Wynne Ruston)的评论《反对詹姆斯·乔伊斯的舆论》(*The Case Against James Joyce*)在《普通人》上发表。 7月,莫顿 D.扎贝尔(Morton D. Zabel)的评论《詹姆斯·乔伊斯的抒情诗》(*The Lyrics of James Joyce*)在《诗》(*Poetry*)上发表。 7月和8月,詹姆斯·乔伊斯先住在伦敦,后住在牛津,又住在威尔士的兰迪德诺镇(Llandudno)。 8月2日,斯图尔特·吉伯特的评论《巨人的成长》(*The Growth of a Titan*)——有关詹姆斯·乔伊斯成长的文章——在《周末文学评论》(*Saturday Review of Literature*)上发表。

9月27日,詹姆斯·乔伊斯致信哈里特·肖·韦弗,把大卫·赫伯特·劳伦斯(David Herbert Lawrence,1885—1930)的长篇小说《查泰莱夫人的情人》(*Lady Chatterley's Lover*,1928)称作《话匣子夫人的情人》(*Lady Chatterbox's Lover*)。

1930年第三季度,蒙哥马利·贝利镇(Montgomery Beligion)的评论《乔伊斯先生和吉伯特先生》(*Mr. Joyce and Mr. Gilbert*)在《本季度》上发表。

11月29日,杰弗里·格里格森(Geoffrey Grigson)的评论《再论詹姆斯·乔伊斯》(*James Joyce again*)在《周末评论》(*Saturday Review*)上发表。

12月,爱德华·W.泰特斯(Edward W. Titus)的评论《乔伊斯先生讲解》(*Mr. Joyce Explains*)在《本季度》上发表。

12月,斯图尔特·吉伯特的评论《乔伊斯式主角》(*The Joycean Protagonist*)在《交流》上发表。

12月,25岁的乔治亚·乔伊斯娶35岁的海伦·卡斯托尔·弗莱施曼(Helen Kastor Fleischmann)为妻。

12月,西尔维奥·本科(Silvio Benco)的评论《詹姆斯·乔伊斯在的里雅斯特》(*James Joyce in Trieste*)在《文人》上发表。

《子孙满天下》(*Haveth Childers Everywhere*)以著作形式由下列两个出版社出版:巴黎的亨利·巴布和杰克·卡亨出版社(Henry Babou and Jack Kahane);纽约的喷泉出版社(The Fountain Press)。

《安娜·利维娅·普卢拉贝勒》由伦敦费伯和费伯书屋(Faber and Faber)出版。

斯图尔特·吉伯特的专著《詹姆斯·乔伊斯的〈尤利西斯〉》(*James Joyce's 'Ulysses'*)由伦敦费伯和费伯书屋出版。

1931年
(49岁)

1931年春,斯图尔特·吉伯特的评论《〈进行中的工作〉的脚注》(*A Footnote to Work in Progress*)在剑桥《实验》(*Experiment*)上发表,对《进行中的工作》做了解释。

3月,迈克尔·莱农(Michael Lennon)的评论《詹姆斯·乔伊斯》(*James Joyce*)在《天主教世界》(*Catholic World*)上发表。

4月,詹姆斯·乔伊斯在威斯巴登(Wiesbaden)逗留了几天。

5月5日,弗雷德里克·勒菲弗(Frederick Lefevre)的评论《詹姆斯·乔伊斯之误》(*l'Erreur de James Joyce*)在《共和国》(*La République*)上发表。

5月,詹姆斯·乔伊斯赴伦敦。

5月,《安娜·利维娅·普卢拉贝勒》法译本在《新法国评论》上发表。

6月10日,约瑟·沃伦·比奇(Joseph Warren Beach)的评论《从詹姆斯到乔伊斯的小说》(*The Novel from James to Joyce*)在《民族》上发表。

7月4日，詹姆斯·乔伊斯与诺拉·巴那克尔在肯辛顿（Kensington）登记结婚。

9月，詹姆斯·乔伊斯离开伦敦赴巴黎。

12月，阿代尔基·巴朗特（Adelchi Barantono）的评论《乔伊斯现象》（*Il Fenomeno Joyce*）在《现代公民》（*Civilia Moderna*）上发表。

12月29日，詹姆斯·乔伊斯的父亲在都柏林去世。

《子孙满天下》由伦敦费伯和费伯书屋出版。

艾德蒙·威尔逊的评论《詹姆斯·乔伊斯》（*James Joyce*）被收入专著《阿克塞尔的城堡：1870年至1930年想象文学研究》（*Axel's Castel：A Study in the Imaginative Literature of 1870－1930*），该书由纽约的查尔斯·斯克里布纳之子出版社（Charles Scribner's Sons）出版。

爱德华·迪雅尔丹（Édouard Dujardin, 1861—1949）的《内心独白：它的外部特征、起源及在詹姆斯·乔伊斯作品中的作用》（*Le Monologue intérieure：son Apparition，ses Origines，sa Place dans l'Oeuvre de James Joyce*）在巴黎发表。

1932年 （50岁）	2月15日，斯蒂芬·詹姆斯·乔伊斯出生，他是乔治亚·乔伊斯和海伦·乔伊斯的长子，也是詹姆斯·乔伊斯的长孙。

2月19日，詹姆斯·乔伊斯创作《瞧这孩子》（*Ecce Puer*）。

2月27日，詹姆斯·乔伊斯的评论《从被禁作家到被禁歌手》（*From a Banned Writer to a Banned Singer*）在伦敦的《新政治家与民族》（*The New Statesman and Nation*）上发表。

3月4日，詹姆斯·乔伊斯给托马斯·斯特恩斯·艾略特写了一封信，谈及《尤利西斯》在美国的出版问题。

3月，托马斯·麦克格林（Thomas McGreevy）的评论《向詹姆斯·乔伊斯致敬》（Homage to James Joyce）在《变迁》上发表。

3月，詹姆斯·乔伊斯的女儿露西娅·乔伊斯患精神分裂症。

玛丽·科拉姆（Mary Colum）的评论《詹姆斯·乔伊斯写照》（*Portrait of James Joyce*）在《都柏林杂志》（*The Dublin Magazine*）上发表。

5月，埃蒙·德·瓦莱拉（Eamon de Valera，1882—1975）被选为爱尔兰自由邦行政委员会主席。

5月22日，爱尔兰剧作家以及阿比剧院的创建人之一格雷戈里夫人去世。

自7月至9月，乔伊斯一家旅居苏黎世。

9月，瑞士著名心理学家兼精神病学家卡尔·古斯塔夫·荣格（Carl Gustav Jung, 1875—1961）的评论《尤利西斯：独白》（*Ulysses：ein Monolog*）在柏林《欧洲评论》（*Europäische Revue*）上发表。

过了9月中旬，乔伊斯一家赴尼斯。

保罗·莱昂（Paul Leon）成为詹姆斯·乔伊斯的秘书。

12月，奥德赛出版社在汉堡、巴黎和波洛尼亚（Bologna）出版了无限量版《尤利西斯》。

塞萨尔·阿宾（César Abin）画了一幅詹姆斯·乔伊斯肖像，该肖像的独特性在于它是一个问号形。

《舍姆和肖恩的故事》在伦敦费伯和费伯书屋出版。

查尔斯·C. 达夫（Charles C. Duff）的作品《詹姆斯·乔伊斯和普通读者》（*James Joyce and the Plain Reader*）在伦敦发表。

卡罗拉·翁-威尔克尔（Carola Giedion-Welcker）的评论《詹姆斯·乔伊斯》（James Joyce）在《法兰克福日报》（*Frankfurter Zeitung*）上发表。

1933年 （51岁）	2月6日，詹姆斯·乔伊斯给W. K. 马吉（W. K. Magee）写了一封信，向对方咨询有关乔治·摩尔（George Moore）葬礼的事情。 5月乔伊斯一家赴苏黎世。 7月，詹姆斯·乔伊斯的女儿露西娅·乔伊斯进瑞士尼翁（Nyon）疗养院。 9月，弗兰克·雷蒙德·利维斯（Frank Raymond Leavis，1895—1978）的评论《乔伊斯和〈词的革命〉》（*Joyce and 'The Revolution of the Word'*）在《推敲：季评》（*Scrutiny：A Quarterly Review*）上发表。 12月6日，美国地方法院法官约翰·蒙罗·伍尔西（John Munro Woolsey，1877—1945）作出了关于《尤利西斯》的判决，认定该小说并非是淫秽作品，《尤利西斯》可以在美国出版。 路易斯·戈尔丁（Louis Golding）的专著《詹姆斯·乔伊斯》（*James Joyce*）在伦敦桑顿·巴特沃斯出版社（Thornton Butterworth）出版。
1934年 （52岁）	1月，纽约的兰登书屋（Random House）出版了无限量版《尤利西斯》。 1月，克利夫顿·法迪曼（Clifton Fadiman）的评论《〈尤利西斯〉在美国首发》（*American Debut of Ulysses*）在《纽约》（*New York*）上发表。 2月14日，威廉·特洛伊（William Troy）的评论《斯蒂芬·迪达勒斯与詹姆斯·乔伊斯》（*Stephen Dedalus and James Joyce*）在《民族》（*The Nation*）上发表。 3月，詹姆斯·乔伊斯到格勒诺布尔（Grenoble）、苏黎世和蒙特卡洛（Monte Carlo）旅行。 4月，詹姆斯·乔伊斯创作《易卜生〈群鬼〉后记》（*Epilogue to Ibsen's "Ghosts"*）。 6月1日，詹姆斯·乔伊斯给露西娅·乔伊斯写了一封信，告诉她：他会想办法，出版《乔叟入门》（*Chaucer's ABC*）。 6月，詹姆斯·乔伊斯的作品《米克、尼克和玛姬的笑剧》（*The Mime of Mick，Nick and the Maggies*）以著作形式在海牙出版，它后来成为《为芬尼根守灵》第二卷第一章的开篇。 6月底，詹姆斯·乔伊斯到东部的旅游城镇斯帕（Spa）。

1934 年夏,约翰·波洛克(John Pollock)的评论《〈尤利西斯〉和审查制度》(*Ulysses and censorship*)在《作者》(*The Author*)上发表。

9 月,詹姆斯·乔伊斯到苏黎世和日内瓦。

9 月,露西娅·乔伊斯转至卡尔·古斯塔夫·荣格(Carl Gustav Jung, 1875—1961)诊所。

10 月,阿曼德·佩提让(Armand Petitjean)的评论《詹姆斯·乔伊斯以及世界语言吸收》(*James Joyce et l'Absorption de Monde par le Language*)在马赛的《南方手册》(*Cahiers du Sud*)上发表。

弗兰克·巴奇恩的著作《詹姆斯·乔伊斯以及〈尤利西斯〉创作》(*James Joyce and the Making of "Ulysses"*)在伦敦出版。

1935 年
(53 岁)

1 月底,詹姆斯·乔伊斯从苏黎世回到巴黎。

5 月 25 日,罗伯特·林德(Robert Lynd)的评论《詹姆斯·乔伊斯和新小说》(*James Joyce and the New Kind of Fiction*)发表。

5 月,保罗·埃尔默·摩尔(Paul Elmer More, 1864—1937)的评论《詹姆斯·乔伊斯》(*James Joyce*)在《北美评论》(*American Review*)上发表。

9 月,詹姆斯·乔伊斯在法国北部的一个小城枫丹白露(Fontainebleau)停留了几天。

10 月,《尤利西斯》由纽约限量版俱乐部(Limited Editions Club)出版,该版印刷 1500 册,其插图由亨利·马蒂斯(Henri Matisse)设计。

A. J. A. 沃尔多克(A. J. A. Waldock)的评论《长篇小说中的实验》(*Experiment in the Novel*)被收入他本人的著作《英国文学的一些最新发展:悉尼大学函授异文系列》(*Some Recent Developments in English Literature:A Series of Sydney University Extension Lection*, 1935)中。该著作由悉尼澳大利亚医学出版公司(Medical Publishing Company)出版。

1936 年
(54 岁)

7 月,詹姆斯·乔伊斯的作品《乔叟入门》发表。

8 月 10 日,詹姆斯·乔伊斯给斯蒂芬·乔伊斯(Stephen Joyce)写了一封信,讲述了一则寓言故事。

8 月和 9 月,乔伊斯一家旅居在丹麦,他们在去丹麦的途中曾到过波恩。

10 月 4 日,詹姆斯·乔伊斯给康斯坦丁 P. 柯伦(Constantine P. Curran)写了一封信,向对方征求了一些关于私人财产的意见。

10 月 15 日,詹姆斯·乔伊斯给其岳母写了一封信,提到露西娅·乔伊斯为他的书《乔叟入门》设计了插图。

| 乔伊斯作品中的
凯尔特歌谣

10 月,《尤利西斯》由伦敦博德利·黑德出版公司（The Bodley Head）出版。该版《尤利西斯》共计 1000 册,其中 100 册有作者签名。

12 月,《诗选》（Collected Poems）由纽约黑太阳出版社出版,该诗集包含《一分钱一只的果子》和《瞧这孩子》。

亨利·赛德尔·坎比（Henry Seidel Canby）的作品《七年的收获》（Seven Years' Harvest）在纽约出版。

大卫·戴希斯（David Daiches）的评论《〈尤利西斯〉的重要性》（The Importance of Ulysses）被收入其著作《新文学价值》（New Literary Values,1936）中。该著作在爱丁堡出版。

1937 年 （55 岁）	5 月 23 日,詹姆斯·乔伊斯给托马斯·基奥勒（Thomas Keohler）写了一封信,为收到《献身者之歌》（Songs of a Devotee）向对方表示感谢。

7 月,爱尔兰共和国宪法通过。

8 月,乔伊斯一家旅居苏黎世。

8 月,范德缸（D. G. Van der vat）的评论《〈尤利西斯〉中的父亲》（Paternity in Ulysses）在《英语学习》（English Studies）上发表。

9 月,乔伊斯一家旅居迪拜（Dieppe）。

9 月,无限量版《尤利西斯》由伦敦博德利·黑德出版公司出版。

10 月,詹姆斯·乔伊斯创作的《她讲的故事》（Storiella as She Is Syung）——《为芬尼根守灵》的一个片段——以著作形式由伦敦科维努斯出版社（Corvinus Press）出版。

阿尔芒·珀蒂让（Armand Petitjean）的评论《乔伊斯的意义》（Signification de Joyce）在《英语研究》（Etudes Anglaises）上发表。

迈尔斯 L. 汉利（Miles L. Hanley）主编的著作《詹姆斯·乔伊斯的〈尤利西斯〉词索引》（Word Index to James Joyce's "Ulysses"）由威斯康星大学出版社出版。

1938 年 （56 岁）	7 月,道格拉斯·海德被选为爱尔兰总统。

自 8 月至 9 月,詹姆斯·乔伊斯和他家人先后旅居苏黎世和洛桑。

11 月,詹姆斯·乔伊斯写完《为芬尼根守灵》。

1939 年 （57 岁）	1 月,威廉·巴特勒·叶芝谢世。

2 月 2 日,詹姆斯·乔伊斯展示了《为芬尼根守灵》的第一个装订本。

4 月 4 日,詹姆斯·乔伊斯给利维娅·斯韦沃（Livia Svevo）写了一封信,谈及一些生活琐事,如：他很挂念弟弟等。

5 月 1 日,雅克·梅尔坎托（Jacques Mercanto）的评论《为芬尼根守灵》（Finnegans Wake）在《新法兰西评论》（Nouvelle Revue Française）上发表。

5月4日,《为芬尼根守灵》由以下两家出版社正式出版:伦敦费伯和费伯出版有限公司(Faber and Faber Limited);纽约海盗出版社(The Viking Press)。

5月5日,哈罗德·尼科尔森(Harold Nicolson)的评论《乔伊斯先生无解的寓言之谜》(*The Indecipherable Mystery of Mr. Joyce's Allegory*)在伦敦《每日电讯报》(*Daily Telegraph*)上发表。

5月8日,布鲁顿·拉斯科(Bruton Rascoe)的评论《为芬尼根守灵》(*Finnegans Wake*)在《新闻周刊》(*Newsweek*)上发表。

5月19日,安东尼·伯特伦(Anthony Bertram)的评论《对乔伊斯先生的看法》(*Views on Mr. Joyce*)在《旁观者》(*Spectator*)上发表。

5月20日,L. J. 菲尼(L. J. Feeney)的评论《詹姆斯·乔伊斯》(*James Joyce*)在《美洲》(*America*)上发表。

6月3日,福特·马道克斯·福特(Ford Madox Ford)的评论《为芬尼根守灵》(*Finnegans Wake*)在《周末文学评论》上发表。

6月10日,保罗·罗森菲尔德(Paul Rosenfeld)的评论《为芬尼根守灵》(*Finnegans Wake*)在《周末文学评论》上发表。

6月28日,埃德蒙·威尔逊(Edmund Wilson)的评论《H. C. 埃里克和家》(*H. C. Earwicker and Family*)在《新共和》上发表。

7月7日,巴里·伯恩(Barry Byrne)的评论《为芬尼根守灵》(*Finnegans Wake*)在《公益》(*Commonweal*)上发表。

7月12日,埃德蒙·威尔逊的评论《H. C. 埃里克的梦》(*The Dream of H. C. Earwicker*)在《新共和》上发表。

7月,乔伊斯一家旅居法国海滨小城埃特勒塔(Étretat)

8月27日,丽奈特·罗伯茨(Lynette Roberts)的评论《为芬尼根守灵》(*Finnegans Wake*)在布宜诺斯艾利斯的《民族》(*La Nacion*)上发表。

8月,乔伊斯一家旅居伯尔尼(Berne)。

9月1日,欧文·B.麦圭尔(Owen B. McGuire)的评论《为芬尼根守灵》(*Finnegans Wake*)在《公益》上发表。

自9月至12月,乔伊斯一家返回法国,住在拉波勒(La Baule)。

10月,阿奇博尔德·希尔(Archibald Hill)的评论《语言学家看〈为芬尼根守灵〉》(*A Philologist Looks at Finnegans Wake*)在《弗吉尼亚季评》(*Virginia Quarterly Review*)上发表。

12月,乔伊斯一家离开巴黎赴维希(Vichy)附近的圣热朗-勒-多姆(St Gérand-le-Puy)。

赫伯特·戈尔曼的著作《詹姆斯·乔伊斯》(*James Joyce*)在纽约出版。

哈里·列文(Harry Levin)写的有关《为芬尼根守灵》的评论《论初览〈为芬尼根守灵〉》(On First Looking into *Finnegans Wake*)发表在《散文和诗歌中的新方向》(*New Directions in Prose and Poetry*)上。

| 乔伊斯作品中的
凯尔特歌谣

大卫·戴希斯(David Daiches)的著作《长篇小说和现代世界》(*The Novel and the Modern World*，1939)由芝加哥大学出版社(University of Chicago Press)出版，该书中的若干部分对詹姆斯·乔伊斯的长篇小说做了评论。

詹姆斯 K.费布尔曼(James K. Feibleman)的评论《神话喜剧：詹姆斯·乔伊斯》(*The Comedy of Myth*：*James Joyce*)被收入《喜剧赞》(*In Praise of Comedy*，1939)中。该书由伦敦的艾伦和昂温出版社(Allen and Unwin)出版。

1940年 (58岁)	6月，巴黎落入阿道夫·希特勒(Adolf Hitler，1889—1945)之手。 12月，詹姆斯·乔伊斯带其家人离开圣热朗-勒-多姆到苏黎世。 赫伯特·戈尔曼的著作《詹姆斯·乔伊斯》(*James Joyce*)由纽约莱因哈特公司(Rinehart)出版。
1941年 (59岁)	1月13日，詹姆斯·乔伊斯因溃疡穿孔在苏黎世红十字护士基地(Schwesterhaus vom Roten Kreuz)逝世。 1月15日，詹姆斯·乔伊斯葬在苏黎世弗林贴隆公墓(Fluntern Cemetery)。

编译者后记

　　英汉双语编译著作《乔伊斯作品中的凯尔特歌谣》为教育部社会科学基金课题"2017年度国别与区域研究中心（备案）：爱尔兰研究中心"（GQ17257）阶段性成果、上海对外经贸大学2020年"内涵建设-学位点建设-国际学术会议"最终成果、国际商务外语学院2020年度内涵建设计划任务最终成果。

　　本课题成果由上海对外经贸大学爱尔兰研究中心（Irish Studies Centre, SUIBE）组织，属于该中心翻译团队的系列笔译实践产物。该中心自成立以来，走理论研究与学术实践相结合的道路，旨在以研究爱尔兰文学研究和作品翻译为基础，进而探究爱尔兰文化、历史、经济等领域，加强该校与爱尔兰高校之间的学术交流。

　　该译作是团队智慧及合作的结晶。此研究团队主要由教师和在读研究生组成。该团队成员利用业余时间，多次聚会，制定翻译计划，查找资料，统一格式，讨论翻译疑难，反复校对，联系出版事宜等，勾绘出一条时光的印迹，写就了一曲苦中作乐的求索之歌。

　　作为上海对外经贸大学爱尔兰研究中心主任、本翻译团队组织者、本编译成果的第一责任人，本人谨向所有参加翻译和校对的合作者致谢！感谢上海对外经贸大学各部门的支持！感谢上海三联书店的责任人以及本书责任编辑宋寅悦先生！

　　在翻译过程中，本人遇到不同语种疑难时，请教了多位专业人士，对他们深怀感激之心。

　　感谢本人的老同学、杰出翻译家、复旦大学德语专家吴勇立博士！

　　感谢本人的同事、上海对外经贸大学优秀学者毛锋副教授！

　　感谢我的优秀弟子、多语种天才、企业家冯雷先生！

　　同时，也感谢帮我查阅资料、解决电脑问题、协助我解决诸多翻译琐事的在读研究生许运巧同学、郭曜宇同学、潘晨亮同学、罗芝晴同学！

当然，必须感谢本人妻子李春梅的理解和支持。为了科研，本人常以本校宾馆或办公室为家，几乎没有分担家务，也很少与家人共享假期。

但愿，此书为未来乔伊斯作品的翻译和研究提供参考。

翻译过程中，主要参考了如下资料：

Abrams，M. H. *A Glossary of Literary Terms*. 7th ed. Beijing：Foreign Language Teaching and Research Press，2004.

Achtemeier，Paul J.，ed. *The HarperCollins Bible Dictionary*. New York：HarperCollins Publishers Inc.，1996.

Beja Morris ed. *James Joyce："Dubliners" and "A Portrait of the Artist as a Young Man."* London：The MacMillan Press Ltd.，1973.

Ellmann，Richard. *James Joyce*. Rev. ed. Oxford：Oxford University Press，1982.

Feng Jianming. *The Transfigurations of the Characters in Joyce's Novels*. Beijing：Foreign Languages Press，2005.

Joyce，James. *Finnegans Wake*. New York：Penguin Books，1976.

—. *Letters of James Joyce*. Ed. Stuart Gilbert. New York：The Viking Press，1957.

—. *Selected Letters of James Joyce*. Ed. Richard Ellmann. New York：The Viking Press，1975.

—. *Stephen Hero*. Ed. Theodore Spencer. Rev. ed. London：The Alden Press，1956.

—. *The Critical Writings of James Joyce*. Ed. Ellsworth Mason and Richard Ellmann. New York：The Viking Press，1959.

—. *The Portable James Joyce*. Ed. Harry Levin. New York：Penguin Books，1976.

—. *Ulysses*. Ed. Hans Walter Gabler，with Wolfhard Stepe and Claus Melchior，and an Afterword by Michael Groden. The Gabler Edition. New York：Random House，Inc.，1986.

Joyce，Stanislaus. *My Brother's Keeper：James Joyce's Early Years*. New York：The Viking Press，1969.

McHugh，Roland. *Annotations to "Finnegans Wake."* 3rd. ed. Baltimore and London：The Johns Hopkins University Press，2006.

《不列颠百科全书》（国际中文版，20 卷）。北京：中国大百科全书出版社，2002 年。

郭国荣主编：《世界人名翻译大辞典》。北京：中国对外翻译出版社，1993 年。

冯建明：《乔伊斯长篇小说人物塑造》。北京：人民文学出版社，2010 年。

冯建明主编：《爱尔兰的凯尔特文学与文化研究》。北京：人民文学出版社，2016 年。

——：《爱尔兰作家和爱尔兰研究》。上海：上海三联书店，2011 年。

詹姆斯·乔伊斯：《看守我兄长的人》，冯建明、张晓青、梅叶萍等译。上海：上海三联书店，2019 年。

——：《流亡者》，冯建明、梅叶萍等译。上海：上海三联书店，2020 年。

——：《斯蒂芬英雄：〈艺术家年轻时的写照〉初稿的一部分》，冯建明、张亚蕊等译。上海：上海三联书店，2019 年。

《圣经》（启导本）。香港：香港海天书楼，2003 年。

夏征农主编：《辞海》[1999 年版缩印本（音序）]。上海：上海辞书出版社，2002 年。

周定国主编：《外国地名译名手册》（中型本）。北京：商务印书馆，1993 年。

冯建明

上海对外经贸大学

教育部国别与区域研究中心爱尔兰研究中心

2020 年冬

图书在版编目(CIP)数据

乔伊斯作品中的凯尔特歌谣/冯建明等编译.—上海:上海三联书店,2022.9
ISBN 978-7-5426-7881-2

Ⅰ.①乔… Ⅱ.①冯… Ⅲ.①乔埃斯(Joyce,James 1882—1941)-文学研究②民间歌谣-文学研究-爱尔兰
Ⅳ.①I562.077

中国版本图书馆 CIP 数据核字(2022)第 187131 号

乔伊斯作品中的凯尔特歌谣

编 译 者 / 冯建明 等

责任编辑 / 宋寅悦
装帧设计 / 一本好书
监　　制 / 姚　军
责任校对 / 王凌霄

出版发行 / 上海三联书店
　　　　(200030)中国上海市漕溪北路 331 号 A 座 6 楼
邮　　箱 / sdxsanlian@sina.com
邮购电话 / 021-22895540
印　　刷 / 上海惠敦印务科技有限公司

版　　次 / 2022 年 9 月第 1 版
印　　次 / 2022 年 9 月第 1 次印刷
开　　本 / 710mm×1000mm　1/16
字　　数 / 200 千字
印　　张 / 20.25
书　　号 / ISBN 978-7-5426-7881-2/I·1792
定　　价 / 68.00 元

敬启读者,如发现本书有印装质量问题,请与印刷厂联系 021-63779028